Neverwrong

The Enchanted Journey Book Three

ROSA LEE JUDE

Rosa Lee Jude

Visit my website at www.RosaLeeJude.com

Books by Rosa Lee Jude

The Enchanted Journey Series
TREMBLE
JASMINE
NEVERWRONG

The Legends of Graham Mansion Series
(with Mary Lin Brewer)
REDEMPTION
AMBITION
DECEPTION
SALVATION
REVELATION

Chapter One

"Hi, Mom."

Tremble smiled as Dana's face appeared on the screen of her tablet. Her mother looked like she had gotten very little sleep.

"Oh, I'm so glad to hear from you. I've been so worried. Neither CeCe nor Bridget have heard from you or Laken in days."

The mention of Laken's name made a wave of sadness pass over Tremble. Her friend and Protector was now frozen in time in the Garden of Stone in Neverwrong. She feared that his fate was permanent like that of her ancestors, Marcellus and Claudia. Tremble had found her natural mother, Jasmine, as her journey had dictated. In doing so though, it had set off a series of events that led to her Protector finding out that he might be a descendant of the one who sought Tremble, Scordato.

"Mom, it's great to see your face. You are spending too much time worrying. I am fine."

"I'm your mother; worrying is my job. What has happened? Where are you?"

Tremble looked around her as she chose her words of response. A silver fog still hung in the air. It was ominous and foreboding. It overshadowed the multicolored beauty of the landscape that was hidden in the sadness of what had recently occurred.

"Is anyone there with you?"

"I'm here, Tremble. We are not leaving your mother alone."

Bridget's smiling, but concerned, face appeared behind Dana's on the screen.

"That's good. Thank you, Bridget." Tremble hesitated before continuing. "I'm in the Garden of Stone in Neverwrong."

"Oh, my. You've already made it to Neverwrong. That was quick." Tremble watched as Dana turned around to look at Bridget. "Isn't that fast?"

Bridget did not respond to Dana's question. She directed another one at Tremble.

"Have you found Jasmine?"

"Yes, we have. She is safe."

"Tremble, can you speak freely?" Bridget's tone was somber.

"There are unfriendly ears that may be eavesdropping. Where is CeCe?"

"She was summoned by Belladonna a few hours ago. We feared that something had happened."

"Something did. Something happened to Laken."

As Tremble briefly told Bridget and Dana what had transpired since she left, her mind raced with the reality of what her words revealed. This was a sharp turn in the road. Nothing they had done during the previous weeks had prepared her for what she saw happen.

"I had hoped that our suspicions about Laken's parentage were false." Bridget let out a deep sigh. "Belladonna was secretive regarding from which line that his Royal DNA originated."

"If he does descend from Scordato, it is not thought, at this point, it was a deliberate action on Belladonna's part. It would surely have been Scordato's trickery and interference. Regardless, Laken's heart is pure and devoted." Tremble's bottom lip quivered as she tried to fight the emotions building inside her. "His loyalty is resolute. He gave his life for me, for Neverwrong, and its future."

"What will you do now?" Dana's calming voice was just what Tremble needed to strengthen her.

"There is significance to this butterfly pendant." Tremble pulled it up to where Dana could see it. "When Laken put on the one that had belonged to Amadeus, everything changed. It contains great power."

"So, Inezia had possession of Amadeus' pendant all of these years?" Bridget asked from the background. "History told us that she was a sly one—smart and resilient. Few would have imagined that she still exists in our realm."

"Yes. It isn't clear to me how she stayed hidden."

"Inezia must possess great power. Her powers of concealment are certainly proof." Bridget paused. Tremble could not see what she was doing. "CeCe shall be returning soon. We will not reveal what you have told us to Belladonna. Jasmine is fully capable of contacting her sister if she wishes."

"You still haven't told us what your next plan of action is." Dana's comment drew Tremble back to the immediate situation.

"The pendants possess great power. The one I am wearing was originally Perpetua's. Forrest wears the one that belonged to Baldric. I think combining the two of them will create a special force. I am the only one who can do that."

"Very interesting, Tremble." Bridget took the tablet out of Dana's grasp. "That could constitute enough force to overthrow Scordato's powers, especially since he does not possess his own necklace."

"Exactly. So, Jasmine and I are going to go and seek out Forrest."

"You said that he is being held by Scordato. That means you have to find *him*, too."

Dana's voice sounded anxious as she took the tablet back from Bridget. The action caused Bridget to bring the screen to life in front of them, giving Tremble a view of both of them.

"That's right, Mom. It's the only way. I think if I gain possession of both Perpetua's and Baldric's pendants, I can undo all that Scordato has done."

"It's not just what Scordato has done." Jasmine came up behind Tremble and enlarged the screen. "I believe that as bad as Scordato is, he is a pawn. He's a pawn for The Evil that Marcellus and Claudia fled from in their original homeland."

"Jasmine is correct. The Evil that we escaped makes Scordato look like an amateur." Inezia also joined the conversation. "Bridget, I am honored to meet you. The service that you and CeCe have given to the Royal Family of Neverwrong has been resilient and extraordinary. Dana, there are no words to describe the love we have for you and the unconditional devotion you have given to Jasmine's child. There is no greater love than a parent for a child."

"I will agree and it is that love that has my hackles of concern rising. No one said that Tremble would go in search of Scordato." Dana's tone was anything but friendly.

"Dana, I thoroughly understand your concern. I share it."

Jasmine moved closer to the screen so that she was virtually eye-to-eye with Dana. "The only reason I am allowing this is because I will be accompanying Tremble. We shall face this force together. From what Tremble has told me, Scordato, in one form or another, has come in contact with her several times throughout her life. Despite our stringent endeavors for protection, he has had ample opportunity to harm her."

"That was then. This is now."

"Yes, I'm afraid that a confrontation is inevitable. Here's the difference. We are going to go and seek out Tremble's father. I shall be with her. The strength of our power together is more than enough to overcome whatever Scordato has to offer."

"Dana, when Tremble was born, Jasmine and Forrest had no way of knowing that the true threat to Tremble's and Neverwrong's future is not Scordato." Inezia addressed Dana. "As powerful as our little Amadeus has grown to be, his fuel comes from a source that would have no issues with disposing of him. This one, The Evil is the true threat to Tremble."

"If that is supposed to relieve my fears, it isn't working."

"Your fears are well-founded, my fine lady. I just want to clarify the source. Tremble shall be far safer to encounter Scordato and The Evil behind him if both her powerful parents are in her company. The only way to insure that is to go and find Forrest."

Tremble watched as Dana pondered what had been said. She wished she could minimize her fears. The reality was that Tremble's own fears were more pronounced than what her mother was verbalizing.

"I have to face this. It is *my* destiny, remember? I can run from this, but I cannot hide. I need to face it head-on with as much reinforcement as possible. You and Dad raised me to face my problems head-on."

Tremble saw a look of resolution pass over Dana's face.

"She is right, Dana. You and Andrew raised her to have this level of confidence." Jasmine smiled tenderly at Dana. "She did not inherit this from Forrest and I; she learned to be brave from you and Andrew."

"They were brave every day of their lives." Bridget put her arm around Dana. "It was a brave thing to raise a magical child."

"A child who was being chased by unimaginable forces of evil. You know that is how you raised me. Now it is time to see what I have learned."

Tremble stopped and reached her hands out toward Dana. Her mother automatically did the same.

"We are worlds apart now." Dana's words brought a tear to Tremble's eyes.

"Not in here." Tremble put her hand over her heart. "Never in here."

"I EXPECTED THE journey to find you to be more complicated."

They decided to get a little rest. Inezia had stayed in the Garden of Stone while Jasmine took Tremble into the Library. For the first time, Tremble was physically within the room she had seen so many times.

"It would have been if Laken hadn't been so smart."

"I don't understand."

"The clues could have led you on several different paths. It would have ultimately taken you to the museum and to Gallery 555." Jasmine shook her head and smiled. "Laken bypassed the others and helped you find the shortest route."

Tremble returned the smile as she remembered how quickly Laken turned the phrase "eggs at 555 Met" into a trip to the Metropolitan Museum of Art to see Fabergé eggs in Gallery 555.

"His powers of deduction are fabulous." Tremble caught the tense of what she had said and her smile turned to a frown.

"You have only known him for a few weeks. I watched him from afar for his entire life. His devotion to you is unshakeable. Most of his waking hours were spent learning about the world where you grew up and where we are now. He knew he needed as much knowledge of both to be able to help you."

"If you knew that, why did you go through all of the twists and turns of a puzzle? Why didn't you just tell him? Was it because you suspected that he had a connection to Scordato?"

"No, it was a much simpler reason, an emotional one. I was afraid that his devotion to being your Protector might also turn into something else."

"Something else?"

"I was afraid his loyal devotion might turn into love."

The words weren't a complete shock to Tremble. She had seen the attentive looks Laken gave her. It was one of the reasons she started becoming forceful and authoritative with him.

"Do you think it has?"

"Do you want it to?"

Tremble paused and stared at Jasmine as she contemplated the question. She searched her heart for what her true feelings were.

"I feel such a connection to Laken. It's deep and meaningful. I think it is a permanent connection, if that is still possible. Yet, it does not quite feel romantic, not in the traditional sense. It feels like it is more familial."

"A bond."

"Yes, a bond that wasn't created, it was always there. A love that shall be different from any other that I experience."

"Remember those words, hold on to that feeling. This could be the key to saving Laken from whatever has hold of him now."

They were quiet, solemn in their individual thoughts. After a while, Tremble noticed that Jasmine was sleeping. She took the opportunity to move closer to her mother and examine the features of the woman who had given her life.

Her porcelain skin was flawless. Tremble saw that upon closer scrutiny there were soft lines around her eyes. Lines of worry, Dana would call them. The mother that raised her had the same ones. Long curling eyelashes of the deepest ebony lay at the bottom of her lids. Tremble imagined the beautiful eyes that they now hid. Two jewels of color that were indescribable in their shade of sparkling blue. Her ebony hair lay in ringlets across her shoulders. She was a sleeping beauty.

From the corner of Tremble's eye, she saw a movement. As she stood up from where she was kneeling, Tremble realized that it wasn't movement exactly. Walking closer, it became clear that one of the books in the ancient section of the Library was glowing. The golden spine of the book was shimmering with sparkles. It appeared to be alive. It was beckoning her.

The shelf it sat on was beyond Tremble's reach. She moved a stool from the corner to the location. Climbing up to the shelf, Tremble began speaking out loud to the book.

"You seem to want my attention."

Her whispered voice stirred Jasmine a little. Tremble stood still for a moment as the sleeping woman moved in her chair. Her eyes remained closed.

Satisfied that Jasmine was still sleeping, Tremble returned her gaze to the bookshelf and reached for the glowing book. As her fingers touched its spine, the whole shelf of books lit up in a similar glow and Tremble felt herself being pulled into the light that surrounded them. She heard a scream come from Jasmine as she was swallowed up.

The hole Tremble was falling down was quite different from her prior experience with Laken. She felt like she was travelling in slow motion. The air around her kept changing temperature. At first it felt cool and damp; then it changed to a dry and warmer feeling. The weather was not the only thing that changed.

The atmosphere around her was in colors that were morphing from one to another. It was a spiraling effect. Light bright shades of spring changed to dramatic neon hues. Then those changed again to dark and dreary colors. All the colors were vivid. Tremble felt like she was floating in different directions. She didn't realize that she was holding something in one hand until her butt hit something hard and the object was almost knocked out of her grasp. It was the book.

Tremble looked around her surroundings and saw nothing, absolutely nothing. She was in a place completely devoid of color, objects, or anything resembling any of the worlds she had experienced. There was nothing except her and the book. She looked down at her hand. The book was still glowing. It didn't make a sound, yet she felt like it was speaking to her.

"Maybe you can tell me where I am?"

Her voice echoed like she was in a deep hole. Nothing around her indicated that, but, the sound was deceiving her nonetheless. Tremble paused for a moment and took a deep breath. Amazingly, she was not afraid. A feeling of calm and comfort surrounded her. She looked again at the book.

"You are going to keep glowing until I open you, aren't you?"

Again, Tremble felt like she heard an answer in her head.

She ran her fingers down the spine and felt the power that was contained within. The sparks tickled her fingertips. Slowly, she opened the book. The glow grew brighter. She had not read the words before Tremble felt herself being pulled inside.

Chapter Two

TREMBLE WAS CATAPULTED into what appeared to be a large old dining room. A long table, as big as she had ever seen, was filled with all sorts of strange looking food. As her eyes adjusted to the scene, she realized there were people sitting around the table. Tremble stepped back, trying to hide herself.

"There is no reason for you to conceal yourself."

Tremble jumped as she turned in the direction of the voice. It was Inezia.

"How did you—"

"I was able to take this journey with you because I have brought you here. This is my homeland. These people were my friends. They were your family." Inezia walked closer to the table.

"Were? Have we travelled back in time?"

"No, we are in the present. Come here and look at them closely."

Slowly, Tremble walked toward the table. As she got closer, she realized the horror of what she saw.

"They are all like Claudia and Marcellus. They are like Laken." Tremble walked from chair to chair. "But, they are not in stone." She turned to see Inezia wipe tears from her face.

"No, the stone state is reserved for your homeland. I believe it is meant to show a permanence in the spell's magic. What you see here is a state of limbo."

"You mean?"

"I mean that these dear people are trapped. We have every reason to believe that they can hear us and see us."

"Oh, that is horrible. How long have they been this way?"

Tremble's gaze drifted back to the table. This time, she looked into the eyes of those she saw there. While glassy in appearance, there was something that she now noticed that seemed to indicate there was still life behind the frozen gaze.

"Hundreds of years. I have stopped counting. It is unbearable to do so."

"This is the world that Claudia and Marcellus came from? This is where most of the Royal siblings were born?"

"Yes. This is our homeland."

"The house appears to be very grand and very old. Is there a system of royalty here as well?"

"No, not like you have seen. We were all equal and all comfortable. Our powers were used here to make everyone's life good. Your family lived in this castle. An equally magnificent one down the road was my home."

"Why am I here? Why have you brought me to see this horror?"

"I am the one who controls the ancient books in the Library. The books belong to me, to my family. I brought them when I fled with Claudia and Marcellus. I want you to see The Evil that is behind everything you are facing. The boy I knew as Amadeus became Scordato because of The Evil that has these people in this state. Scordato is a pawn, a powerful pawn."

Tremble's eyes filled with tears of frustration as she paced around the table looking at each person seated there.

"No matter how much everyone tells me, I still do not understand how I am supposed to combat all of this. I don't understand what it all means."

"Come outside with me."

Inezia began walking out of the room so quickly that Tremble had trouble keeping up with the older woman. She was not sure if Inezia's feet were touching the ground. As they walked out of the dining room and down a massive hallway, Tremble tried to take in her surroundings. Everything was grey and dark. It felt like she was in a haunted castle. From what she had just seen, it was an accurate description.

Tremble was so intent on the surroundings that she almost walked into Inezia as the woman stood in the middle of a grand foyer with a high ceiling. A light from above drew her eye. The light came down through a large stained glass skylight. Tremble could not make out the exact design, but thought she saw small birds depicted.

Her gaze followed the light down to the floor. As her eyes adjusted, she saw that they were standing on a marble floor within a large circle. Around the edges of the circle were butterflies of all different colors. Her eye caught a purple one. As she bent down to get a closer look, Tremble realized that it was the same one that hung around her neck. She stood back up and counted. There were eight butterflies.

"Yes, this is my work. I am the Keeper of the Butterflies in this world."

"What is the name of this kingdom?"

From the direction that Inezia's arms were going, Tremble could see that she was beginning a spell to open the massive doors in front of them. She stopped and quickly turned to face Tremble.

"I cannot say the name. It will summon THE EVIL. The Evil that rose up from our very core and aims to destroy us. You know what happened to Amadeus. The story of what went wrong in this world I call my home is a similar tale. History is repeating itself. It is why it is so important to stop it. I cannot say the name until that happens."

Tremble watched as Inezia turned back to the door. Again her arms were lifted and from her fingertips shot sparks of fuchsia. The force made the massive doors fling open and the resulting wind knocked Tremble to the floor. As she steadied herself to rise, Tremble felt the twitch of a butterfly wing underneath her hand.

"This is what happens when hope dies."

Tremble rose and followed Inezia onto the long rectangular porch in front of the castle. As far as the eye could see, everything was glazed in a sad shade of yellow. It reminded her of mustard, yet not quite as bright.

"This is the color of melancholy. It is the manifestation of what happens when you become so sad that even sadness is an effort. This world has been like this for hundreds of years now. Once upon a time, though, it looked like this."

Tremble watched as the old woman bent down and gradually pulled up her arms to the sky. She couldn't make out the words that Inezia was mumbling. There was no doubt of their power. Tremble was awestruck as all of the yellow disappeared as if the woman was peeling back a piece of plastic. The colors that came into view were breathtaking and quite familiar. Immediately, Tremble noticed that the colors were similar to the ones she had grown up seeing.

"The sky is blue!" Tremble could not control her enthusiasm. It was wonderful to see normal in her very abnormal life.

"I wondered how long it would take you to notice the difference. This world is much more like the mortal world you grew up in."

"Why the difference?"

Tremble looked out onto the horizon. The view reminded her of many different parts of the mortal world. It seemed as if in each direction that she looked there was a different continent.

"Making Neverwrong different from his homeland was Marcellus' idea. What we had experienced here was so horrid, so tragic, it was his desire to make our new world completely different. It wasn't possible. There are certain things that are consistent across most worlds that exist. If everything had looked the same in Neverwrong as it did in our homeland, it would have been harder to bear that our loved ones were not with us."

Tremble continued to look around while Inezia was speaking. She walked down the long porch and back again. She was about to go down the steps into the yard when she felt a tight grip on her shirt pull her back.

"We cannot leave the porch. If we step off even an inch, we will cease to exist."

Tremble turned back toward the door.

"Again, I've got to ask. Why are we here?"

"You need to see what you are up against. The Evil is more powerful than you can imagine. It has a vengeance that knows no limits. Look at how beautiful this land is."

Tremble looked again at the landscape. She heard Inezia snap her fingers and the ugly yellow hue instantly covered everything.

"How did you do that?"

"I created an illusion to show you the way it was. As you see it now, that's the way it is." Inezia pointed through the doorway. "We shall not linger here any longer. I wanted you to get a glimpse of what was. I want you to understand the severity of change The Evil has caused. This is what The Evil will do to Neverwrong."

As they entered the foyer again, Tremble looked down at the marble floor. All the butterflies were fluttering as if they were glad to see the one who created them.

"Did you create these knowing how many children Marcellus and Claudia would have?"

"Yes, my eyes saw the future in respect to them. I did not see what would happen to them in this world or the next one. I would have surely tried to change it, had I known."

"How could you have done that if The Evil is so powerful?"

"It was not always. Most of its power was drawn from others. All those you saw sitting at the table in there were drained of their power as were Marcellus and Claudia."

"So this being or whatever you call it was not always a powerful evil force?"

"Absolutely not."

"What was it before?"

Tremble watched the look that crossed Inezia's face and the language her body spoke. Her very spirit was deflating like a balloon from which the air was released.

"Once upon a time, it was my husband."

Tremble tried to catch the gasp that came out of her mouth. It was too late.

"What?"

"There's really no time to get into that now. We must return to Neverwrong. Jasmine does not know that I have brought you here. She will not be pleased about it."

With a flick of Inezia's wrist the book reappeared in Tremble's hand.

"Open it. It's time to go."

Tremble did as Inezia said. With a blink of her eye, the book again swallowed her into its grasp. The trip was short and once again, Tremble found herself in the Library. Jasmine was no longer sleeping.

"Would someone care to tell me where the two of you have been?" Jasmine shot Tremble a look before she continued. "Yes, I know that you did not do this on your own. Where did you take my daughter?"

"Calm down, Jasmine. You have the right to be aggravated with me. I should have asked. I didn't because I knew you would not agree to it."

Tremble stood quietly at the same bookshelf where the mini journey had begun. It was out of the way, yet also offered a full view of what she could only imagine was likely to be a heated exchange.

"Your actions should not amaze me."

Jasmine stood up from the chair and walked determinedly toward Inezia. Tremble saw yellow sparks flying from the bottom of the sleeves of Jasmine's multicolored jacket. She noticed the high navy and silver boots that covered the navy pants Jasmine was wearing. The outfit reminded her of one worn while horseback riding. It was more colorful and glamorous than she had ever seen used for that sport. Jasmine had a distinctive style. Tremble wondered what Jasmine had in mind for the next portion of their journey.

"It was just a brief trip. In and out. No harm, no foul. I thought it was important for Tremble to see the land of my birth. It would add to her knowledge to see the outcome of The Evil that she shall now face."

"You took her to—"

"No, my dear, stop! You must not say the word. We cannot risk summoning the power directly in our midst."

"So you say. So legend says. You are the only one who tells this tale, you know."

"I am the only one around to tell the tale. I must protect and guide those who will listen."

Jasmine turned on her heel and faced Tremble.

"So, you saw the place from which our family came. What did you think of it?"

"It was beautiful."

A look of shock and bewilderment crossed Jasmine's face. She turned back to Inezia.

"I thought you said you took her to—"

"I took her there. I also showed her how it once was. As I showed you once, remember?"

"Yes, I had forgotten. That glimpse was one of the things that drew me to the mortal world. I do not understand why our ancestors wanted to create a place so different from it."

"You do not like the natural state of Neverwrong?" Tremble stepped down from the bookshelf area and drew closer to Jasmine.

"I love my homeland. You must remember though, it is not a 'natural state' as you call it. Neverwrong was created by Marcellus. He conjured how it would look, how it would be."

"Isn't that true of the mortal world as well? It was created somehow." Tremble continued questioning her mother.

"I suppose you are right. I do not think that creating a world to be the opposite of another is natural."

Jasmine paused and took hold of the bracelet on her wrist. Tremble watched as her mother opened the face of it and gazed inside before quickly shutting it back.

"You have showed her the results of The Evil. Have you told my dear daughter who this it is?"

"Right before we left, I asked the same thing and Inezia told me it was once her husband. I don't understand."

"So you have spared her the worst part." Jasmine shook her head as she paced the floor in the middle of the Library. "It is all written in some of those books."

Jasmine flicked her hand in the direction of another bookshelf. One or two of the volumes lit up in different colors and flew off the shelves. Jasmine did not seem to notice. The books hovered in the air as she continued talking.

"I am sure that Laken did not tell her that the Neverwrong Royals' story is not far removed from that of our ancestors in—" Jasmine stopped herself and held a finger up to her lips. "Yes, it is a secret. The name is a secret. The story we know. I am sure that dear Belladonna did not include this is Laken's training. Especially, if she had any suspicions to his own origin."

Jasmine sat down in a large straight chair. Tremble's mind reverted back to the first time she had seen the Library. Scordato had made seven similar chairs appear for his siblings to sit in. She wondered if the chair that Jasmine now sat in had remained from that time.

"Are you paying attention, my daughter? Your thoughts seem to be remembering something that you have seen here before."

Tremble tilted her head and stared deeply into Jasmine's eyes.

Their beautiful color was mesmerizing. She wondered if that was part of her mother's power.

"Are you able to read my thoughts? Laken seemed to have some ability in that regard."

"Really? Laken could look inside your mind?"

Jasmine paused for a moment. Tremble could see that those same beautiful eyes were now in a journey of thought as they darted from side to side. Yet, somehow she knew that it was not within the room where they now were that those eyes were searching.

"I think he could to a point. I'm not sure how deep or for how long he could probe. He never told me."

A sudden feeling of sadness overwhelmed Tremble. She was beginning to realize that Laken might be forever gone from her life. It pained her more than she imagined.

"Very well. It is interesting nonetheless. Shall I tell her this sordid tale, Inezia, or would you rather tell it?"

"You only know what you have been told, my dear girl. I know the truth of the matter. I shall tell it. Let us find a more relaxing place than this dreadful room."

Inezia began to lift up her arms, obviously to change their location, when Tremble stopped her.

"Dreadful room? Why is this room dreadful?"

"Can you not feel it, my child?"

Tremble stood perfectly still and tried to absorb the feeling they were mentioning. She felt nothing. "I don't feel anything unusual."

"Tremble, what you have said is interesting to us. This Library is still considered to be Scordato's domain. Even though many successive generations have had access and used this space, it is still very apparent to most of us that he is here, at times."

Inezia paced as she spoke.

"We have developed spells to prevent him from seeing us or hearing our conversations. Like us, he can probably detect our presence. We are sort of renting the same space." Jasmine laughed and her aura sent out a myriad of tiny multicolored sparks. "I did not feel him when we first arrived. While you two were gone, I felt a change. To me, the feeling resembles how the atmosphere changes right before a storm. It's like the air starts getting heavier."

"It is subtler for me." Inezia stopped pacing. "I suppose that is because I knew him and loved him as a child. I feel something akin to a gentle rain in the air. It is not too disturbing as long as it doesn't last too long." Inezia smiled at Tremble. "It's lasted too long now. We must seek another place to stay for a while."

"Oh, Inezia, dare we take her to the tower room?"

"Jasmine, you chastised me for taking her to my homeland, yet you suggest the tower room?"

"It would be a good test. It might prove beneficial to know if we could get in and out undetected. Now that I have my darling girl in my midst, I am ready to take real adventures with her, like a normal magical mother."

Tremble shook her head as she listened to the dialogue between the two.

"What are you laughing at, young lady?" Inezia stood with her hands on her hips. She reminded Tremble of a fairy godmother.

"Jasmine speaks of taking adventures like a normal magical mother. From my perspective, that is a contradiction of terms."

"I understand that. Remember though, you have only known this new perspective of your life for a few weeks. Jasmine has lived it for twenty-one years."

While Tremble realized that Inezia did not intend to sound harsh, her words stung nonetheless. Tremble had not fully considered what all those years of waiting had been like for Jasmine. Her child was out there in another world and she could not experience anything with her.

"I say let's go to the tower room, whatever that is." Tremble gave Jasmine a broad smile. "Let's take my magic out for a spin and see what it can do."

Inezia did not wait for further debate. Her hands went up over her head, and then swept around both Jasmine and Tremble. The swirl of color was awe inspiring. It caught Tremble's breath. Before anyone could say a word, they were instantly in another place.

Chapter Three

"THAT IS ONE thing that Hollywood got right."

Tremble looked down at her body to make sure that all her limbs were still attached. She had felt the movement, yet was amazed at how quickly they had made the trip.

"Whatever do you mean, my dear?"

Inezia was re-adjusting her outfit a little. Tremble noticed that the woman had changed her attire mid-trip. She was now adorned in a long burgundy dress with lots of intricate embroidery. The turned up collar at her neck reminded Tremble of how fairy godmothers were described in the many fairytales she had read as a child.

"Oh, Inezia. You must know of the mortal world's fondness with make believe. There's a whole business built around it in a city called Hollywood." Jasmine smiled as she spoke.

Her outfit had changed as well during their journey. Jasmine was now wearing a long dress similar in style to Inezia's. Hers was solid black with multicolored embroidery all throughout the fabric. As Tremble looked closer, she saw the design on the back of the dress was a peacock.

Tremble began to look around the room. As she did so, she observed that her own attire had changed. Her dress was identical to Jasmine's in style. The color was a deep rich purple. The embroidery was made with a silky black thread. The designs were geometric in shape. She reached for her neck and found the pendant still safely there.

"Do you like it?"

"It is beautiful. But, why have we changed clothes?"

"I could tell you that there is an enchanted reason." Jasmine lifted up the skirt and twirled around. "It wouldn't be true. Our journey from here on out is going to be cloaked in danger. I thought it would be nice for us to look pretty while we travel." Jasmine gave Tremble a wink. "This attire shall also allow us to blend in with our environment. This design is the latest in Neverwrong fashion, a revival of past enchantress style is going on."

As she watched the mischievous grin cross Jasmine's face, Tremble began to see her mother's true personality shine through. Genetics could not be denied. Tremble's whimsical spirit came straight from this woman. It had been nurtured and encouraged by those who had raised her.

Breaking her chain of thought, Tremble again began to look around her. The room they were in was not large. The darkness was broken by high windows that were almost too high for her to look out. The room was circular. The walls were all multicolored with splashes of color like a painting. Tremble reached out and touched one of them. It was a work of art. It had a feeling of wetness, yet, left no paint residue on her fingertips. Stopping at one window, she rose on her toes to look outside. It was daytime. A creamy yellow sky was in clear view. A few soft lavender clouds floated by as the brightness of a blue sun shone behind them.

"We are in Neverwrong, are we not?" Tremble lowered her feet and turned back toward Jasmine.

"Yes. It is a strange feeling for me." Tremble gave her a puzzled look. "I have not been this close to our central city since before you were born. I daresay that Belladonna is twitching all over somewhere below us. She most surely has picked up my presence."

Tremble watched as Jasmine exchanged looks with Inezia. She felt sure that a conversation was going on between them. As she tried to concentrate on them, she began to hear snippets of something. It was like trying to tune in a radio station.

"She will not be pleased that I have not told her." Jasmine's voice came to Tremble in a whispered tone.

"We must be cautious. I do not trust her intent."

"She is my sister, my flesh and blood."

"You are forgetting, my child, those who came before you that denied those of their birth."

Tremble's eyes darted back and forth as she continued to try to listen. She wasn't hearing anything so she looked around and found that Jasmine and Inezia were watching her. Tremble smiled innocently at them.

"Are you okay?" Jasmine walked toward Tremble. "Your aura has turned an unusual color. It indicates you are in fear or you are unwell."

Again, Tremble's eyes began to dart. This time, her mind was searching for how to respond. Her eyes met Inezia's. There was a sly look on the old woman's face. Something told Tremble that she could not hide what had just happened. She turned back to her mother.

"I'm fine. I don't know why my aura looks strange. I don't feel afraid."

"Do not feel like you need to hide your feelings from us, Tremble. We understand that all you are experiencing is foreign to you. We understand if it scares you."

"I know. It's overwhelming. That's not what is happening right now."

Tremble paused and looked back at Inezia. The nod of the woman's head would have been unperceivable to anyone except Tremble.

"Tell us." Inezia's voice was strong.

"I was hearing the conversation between you. I heard what you said about Belladonna."

"Be still, Tremble. Don't speak of this out loud."

Tremble looked at Jasmine as her mother took hold of her arm.

"I don't—"

"You are in another dimension, Tremble." Inezia joined them in the center of the room. "Everyone in this world has great powers of perception. We may not be alone. We understand what you have told us."

"It is good for you to use these powers. Work to make them useful for you. We will help you." Jasmine looked deep into Tremble's eyes. "Understand our words. Be mindful of the implications."

"What is this place? Why are we here?"

"This place is very special, Tremble. It is one of the towers in our family castle. You are now in the palace of the Royal Family of Neverwrong."

Inezia's words shocked Tremble. She understood that she

was in Neverwrong, but being in the royal palace was another story.

"That seems dangerous."

"Why, my dear? This is your family's home." Jasmine tilted her head as she questioned Tremble.

"You went to great lengths to keep me away from here. I thought that meant there was great danger here."

"Well, I suppose you would think that. I was not hiding you from my home. You must now understand that I was hiding you from The Evil that wants to destroy us. It wants to consume our happiness and use it as a power of its own."

"The Evil drove me and your ancestors from our homeland. We are safe now for me to tell you who The Evil really is."

Inezia pulled Tremble down to a bench for them to sit. It was a circular area with plenty of space for the three of them. Jasmine joined by sitting behind Tremble.

"When I was a young girl, a man came to our land, the place that I took you to earlier today. The man was a stranger to our people, but led us to believe that he was from a kingdom in another dimension. He said he had stumbled out of his own world and knew not how to return. The elders of our time engaged him in many discussions and probed him as to how he had made his way to our land. The man did not seem to know. It was as if his memory had left him."

Tremble expected a screen to appear before them. She thought that Inezia would take the memory and put it in movie form for them to see with her. Instead, something even more unusual happened. Just a foot or two before them, a man appeared. He was beautiful.

"This is Sebastian."

Inezia let out a deep sigh and a tremble passed over her. They were sitting so close that the feeling passed through Tremble as well and startled her. She looked at the woman to find that Jasmine had put one arm around her friend.

"He was kind and gentle. He worked and helped others. Time passed and it was as though he had always lived in our kingdom. Sebastian became close to my family, especially my father. He was a trusted part of our lives. I grew into a young woman and he started to look at me differently. He did not know that he had always held my heart."

Her words touched Tremble and she reached for the old woman's hand. In front of them, Sebastian was joined by a beautiful woman, a younger version of Inezia. A circle of light engulfed them as they joined hands. Around that light was a funnel of darkness. Tremble turned and looked at her mother. Jasmine gave her a questioning look in return.

"Inezia, I am sorry to interrupt you. I must ask about the image we see before us. I see light surrounding the two of you."

"Yes, that is correct. That is the light of our love."

"And the darkness that surrounds it, what is that?"

"What darkness? What do you mean?"

"You see something else, Tremble?" Jasmine rose behind them and walked toward where the image was. "You see something more than the light?"

"Yes, I see a funnel of darkness around them. You can't see it?" Tremble stood up as well and walked toward the image on the other side. "It's very pronounced and thick, almost like a wall."

Tremble reached out her hand to touch the image and she heard a blood curdling scream come from Inezia.

"NO! STOP! Tremble, stop!"

In a flash, Jasmine was pushing Tremble to the ground away

from the dark edge of the funnel. Tremble scooted further away until she felt a wall behind her.

"I did not mean to frighten you. If you had—"

"Tremble, stepping into that time, into that place would be like falling down a black hole. You could never return to us."

Inezia reached out her hand. Tremble thought she was going to help her up. She did just that, only with magic. In an instant, Tremble was sitting again next to the old woman and Jasmine was sitting behind them. The image before them had vanished.

"I fell in love with Sebastian. We married. He officially became part of our magical world. Before my very eyes, he rose in power. The elders of our kingdom grew strong in their faith and reliance on his guidance. He became Marcellus' best friend. Claudia and Marcellus had been married shortly before Sebastian and I. Claudia gave birth to the twins, and we were named their godparents. Perpetua was born. Shortly thereafter, I gave birth to a child."

Tremble felt the room grow cold. Even under the long sleeves of her dress, she could feel the hairs on her arms stand straight up. In the distance, she thought she heard an animal howl.

"You have a child?" Inezia had grown silent so Tremble asked the question.

"I had a son. A son I never saw. He was killed by his own father."

"I don't understand." Tremble looked back at Jasmine. Her mother shook her head slightly.

Inezia rose and walked toward one of the windows.

"Sebastian was not from our world. He was not even from a magical world. He was not a being like us, mortal or immortal. He is pure evil." Inezia continued to stare out of the window. "He knew that his offspring would not be what I was expecting to deliver. I had ignored the signs as I carried my child. The pregnancy was short, only four months. My belly was huge. I could not walk for the last month. My dreams were filled with beings that made me wake up screaming. Sebastian tried once to end my life before I had the child. Claudia stopped him. I'm sure that is what spurred what later happened to them. I have no doubt that the fate that waited for Amadeus would have been what Sebastian desired for all of the Royal children."

"What Inezia is trying to tell you is that The Evil we are fighting against is truly Sebastian. That is not his actual name. He put his real name on the kingdom that our ancestors came from when he took it over. That is the reason Inezia does not want it uttered."

"The name is a summons. Were it not for the fact that Amadeus and Baldric had begun to study the books that dealt with that time, he might never have re-entered our lives. Innocently, they read the name aloud from a book and that gave him his entrance into this kingdom. We fled after the worst had happened—after he sucked the power out of all of those we loved and began his mission of destruction."

"Do you think that Scordato learned this and has summoned him since?"

"That is a very good question, Tremble." Jasmine paused and thought before continuing. "We have wondered if Scordato gained his power and abilities purely through the study of the Library, as he has said, or, if power has been bestowed upon him."

"Inezia, you knew these children as well as anyone. You were their nanny, their close companion." Inezia nodded her head affirmatively. "Do you think that Baldric knew that Amadeus was alive when they left him?"

"Oh, my child, that is a question that has haunted me for

hundreds of years. I have searched my heart, and there is no reason for me to believe that Baldric had malice toward his brother. They were rivals, to be sure. Brothers, yes, twins, would have that in their nature. But, that closest of bonds would also have at its root a love deeper than we can imagine. It would be a kinship of their very blood and being." Inezia rose and paced for a few moments before she resumed speaking. "I fear that Baldric's actions were truly based on another emotion—fear. He saw what happened to his beloved parents. He knew that something connected to that had imbedded itself into Amadeus. I believe that Baldric feared for the rest of his family—the dear baby sisters who had his heart."

Tremble found that tears were welling in her eyes. As she considered Inezia's words, it occurred to her what a massive burden had been laid on Baldric's shoulders. She understood such a burden. She bore one now. At least, she was allowed to reach the age of adulthood and understanding before the task of fulfilling it had been revealed to her.

"Forrest, your father, has spoken of this very thing many times." Jasmine's expression was full of love as she spoke of her husband. "Through our youth and early adulthood, he spent many hours in the hall of portraits conversing with Baldric. In their solitary conversations, Baldric opened his heart to this grandson from future generations. His words to Forrest were very much like Inezia's words now. He did not wish harm on his brother. He feared for the safety of the rest of his family."

"Would you sacrifice one sibling to save six others? It is not a question that any of us knows, with certainty, how we would answer. It could have been an unconscious action on Baldric's part. I do know, however, their parents did that very thing. They left the safety of their home in the mountain to confront what they knew had followed them. Marcellus and Claudia knew what their sons had done. They knew the whispered words from innocent mouths had blazed a path to their door."

"Why didn't Sebastian go after the children after turning Marcellus and Claudia into stone? He could have wiped out everyone then."

"You are so wise, my daughter. I see that Dana and Andrew have taught you the power of logical thinking. This woman from generations past that you see before you—this angel of mercy who has hidden me under her power all of these years while I waited for you to grow. Inezia is the reason that the children lived. She is the reason why The Seven were able to go forth and establish the Kingdom of Neverwrong."

Jasmine joined Inezia where she was standing. The two embraced and shared whispered words.

"I encircled those children with a spell to protect them from Sebastian. I made sure that the spell would have the power to follow them to the new kingdom they would form. I did not foresee that they would leave one of their own behind." Inezia paused for a moment. "I have told you that Sebastian did not possess his own powers. Perhaps, you do not understand the full meaning of what I said. He is not an enchanter, a warlock, or a wizard. The land from which he came was devoid of magic. A very wise man among us was able to extract this information from Sebastian once we realized that he was not of good intent. Those who Sebastian descended from had been banished from the magical world eons ago. This did not mean that the people of that land no longer knew of the existence of magic. Quite the contrary. Part of their punishment for a crime long forgotten was their continued knowledge of the existence of magic—what they could not possess."

Inezia left Jasmine's grasp and walked toward Tremble. She sat back down on the center bench and pulled Tremble to her. She took both of Tremble's hands within her own and looked deeply into the young woman's eyes.

"You have been raised in love and wisdom in the mortal world. It is clear that those who surrendered their lives to protect yours had great depths of human wisdom and understanding. Because of this and the infinite powers from which you descended, you should have no trouble understanding what I am about to say. I must admonish you to pay close attention, hear my words, and feel them."

Tremble nodded and kept her gaze firmly locked with Inezia. She could feel the sparks of magical anticipation coming out of her. She wondered what color her aura was.

"It is silver. That represents intense concentration."

Jasmine's sudden comment startled Tremble. She smiled as she realized that their bond and connection was progressing for her mother to so clearly read her thoughts.

"All beings of life have a common spirit. Beings who share intelligence and gendered form also share emotion. I have lived through many years and in several different lands. I have observed even more as I have journeyed into the mortal world. The downfall of a being is never something that is done to it. The downfall comes from within. Those who long for what they do not have while not appreciating what they *do* possess are always cloaked with failure. When you appreciate what is in your grasp, you will always be given more."

"Listen to her words, Tremble. They are the root of everything. They are the secret to all that we know."

"Sebastian rose out of the people of his land because he could only see what he did not have. He wanted the power of magic, even though it would not be possible for him to truly possess it."

"I don't understand. You have said that he stole from the people of your land—he stole their powers. I saw their lifeless forms. Did he take the magic from them?"

"Indeed, he took it. Yet, he still does not possess it. It is the same with Scordato. He blindly followed this evil way. Young Amadeus longed for acceptance. He himself does not know where it came from. Scordato doesn't know that he is in allegiance with the very thing that took all he had away from him. Again, he does not appreciate what he had, only what he did not."

"I understand your words and, yet, I do not. It all seems like a circle that no one can escape from."

"Ah, Jasmine, you are so right! This child possesses the wisdom of the ages. It is just outside her grasp." Inezia turned back to address Tremble. "Yes, both Sebastian and Scordato are in a vicious cycle. Sebastian can never have what his core desire dictates. Scordato, on the other hand, could be saved if his heart would open to see the true source of the pain that drives him."

"Forgiveness. Scordato needs forgiveness. Not to receive, but to give from himself."

"Exactly, my dear. This is why you are the fulfillment of the prophecy."

Before Tremble could respond to what had just been said, a door flew open. She had been so absorbed in what she was being told, Tremble had not examined the room for its entryway.

Through the door walked Belladonna. It shocked Tremble to see CeCe behind her.

Tremble could feel the anger coming from Belladonna. Whatever emotion of relief that the grand enchantress had within her soul for her sister and niece, it was overpowered at that moment by rage. As Tremble caught a glimpse of Belladonna's eyes, she wondered if anyone else could see the glow of red coming from them. The red matched the pendant around her neck. Tremble had seen it previously. Before she could explore the thought any further, a silent message of 'I can' passed through her mind. Jasmine had read her thoughts loud and clear.

"My sister, so long lost, why have you not announced your arrival? I would have thought I would have been the first one you would have informed for the safety of yourself and our precious Tremble."

Belladonna's eyes locked with Jasmine's. Tremble could only imagine that words were being exchanged.

"I did not think it would be prudent to put that knowledge in anyone's grasp. We have not spoken. I did not know your situation." Jasmine broke the eye contact and shifted her gaze "CeCe, what a pleasure to see you again. Your leadership in the protection of Tremble has been stellar."

"Your Royal Highness, it has been my distinct—"

"What in the world am I witnessing here? You are bestowing gratitude on our servants before you embrace the one who has given up everything for—"

It wasn't just Belladonna's eyes that glowed red; her entire aura looked like a fire alarm going off. So intense was its color that Tremble thought she could feel heat coming off of the woman.

"Belladonna, calm yourself. I have come into our family domain, and I have brought my daughter AND our family's dear companion, Inezia. You shall show some respect for all those in our presence. CeCe is far from being a servant. She is a comrade in arms."

Belladonna remained silent. Her aura did not dim.

"As I was saying, my gratitude is immense to the Royal Order of Protectors."

"We *are* your humble servants, Your Royal Highness." CeCe began to walk toward them. Her eyes darted to Tremble.

"Enough of that, CeCe. We were playmates. When all of this is over, I shall rid us of all of this pomp and circumstance once and for all."

"Why, Jasmine, surely you do not mean to abandon the place our family—"

"Belladonna, do not pretend you know what the place of our family should be. It is all vanity. A waste, when real problems exist in the worlds around us."

"Yes, yes. You will want to take us all to the mortal world to fix all that is wrong there. You are the Healer." Belladonna's feelings dripped from her words.

Tremble began to feel a change in the room. It wasn't just the aggression coming from Belladonna. It felt as if the balance in the room was off as two forces were engaged in something that was years in the making.

"We have come here as a test, my dear sister. We have come here to see if we can do so undetected. I am not surprised that you were able to know of my presence. What I want to know is did you detect Tremble?"

The brightness of Belladonna's aura began to diminish as she pondered Jasmine's question. Tremble watched as her aunt began walking toward her. Once she was close enough, Belladonna reached out her arms to Tremble. A hesitance came over Tremble until the whisper of her mother's voice asked her to accept Belladonna's embrace. As she walked toward her aunt, the woman's aura changed completely, it disappeared from view.

Belladonna's arms encircled her and Tremble felt a true embrace from the woman. After a few seconds, Tremble returned the hug and felt Belladonna's embrace tighten and as quickly fall away. For a moment, Tremble felt real love. Yet, she wondered if it was genuine or it had an agenda. Belladonna's guard quickly concealed the emotion. She moved away from Tremble before she could realize what was happening.

"I did not feel her presence. We do not have a connection as you and I do."

"It could be because you have not been this close to her before. You did not have an imprint of her to call upon."

"Perhaps." Belladonna's tone was curt. Tremble watched as the woman fingered the large red diamond pendant that hung around her neck. "Our interactions over the past few weeks should have formed some sort of mark on my perceptions if I was going to be able to detect her. I knew that Inezia was here, and I cannot remember ever being in her physical presence before."

Jasmine walked around the room with her back to Belladonna. After a few minutes passed, Tremble saw CeCe begin to approach her. Tremble watched as CeCe's eyes darted between Jasmine and Belladonna. Both seemed to be lost in their own thoughts.

"Where's Laken?" CeCe's question was barely over a whisper.

The question caused both Jasmine and Belladonna to turn toward her. A small nod from Jasmine told Tremble to answer CeCe.

"Laken is—" Tremble's voice began to crack. Her eyes rose and met Jasmine's. Her gaze was strengthening. Tremble felt herself calm. "Laken is not with us."

"Did something happen to him?" Tremble's response did not

seem to be coming fast enough for CeCe. "Is he okay?" CeCe's brow furrowed to reveal her worry.

"Laken is in the Garden of Stone. He is now like Marcellus and Claudia."

A gasp came out of CeCe's mouth that could only be described as pain. Her whole body began to shake.

"Oh, I felt it. I made my mind ignore it. I knew the moment it occurred. I am more his mother than I realized. His life force is not extinguished. He is still in there." CeCe sank to the floor. Inezia quickly went to her side and embraced her. "His hope rests on you." CeCe's head rose and her eyes met Tremble's. "You are his Protector now. Do you know that?"

"I do."

"Why was I not informed? Laken is my responsibility." The anger returned to Belladonna's voice. "Has everyone forgotten my authority in the matter?"

Jasmine walked toward her sister. She pulled her into what appeared to Tremble to be an awkward embrace. After she released Belladonna, Jasmine held her sister at arm's length with her hands firmly holding Belladonna's wrists. Tremble thought it was an unusual stance.

"My sister, I have appreciated your resolute service on my behalf, on behalf of Forrest, during our absence. But, as the Supreme Ruler of Neverwrong, I did not feel it necessary to inform you of something that occurred in my presence when I knew that I would be seeing you."

As if someone had flipped a switch, the temperature of the room dropped quickly. Tremble felt an icy chill down her spine. An unseen gauntlet had been thrown down.

"Very well, Your Royal Highness." Belladonna shook off Jasmine's hold on her like she was breaking out of handcuffs. "Perhaps, I should go on my own journey and leave the rest of this horrid prophecy business to you and *your* firstborn. An extended holiday throughout our kingdom and its neighbors might be in order before the prophecy is fulfilled and it is no longer in its beautiful state. Before it becomes like the land of Inezia's birth, like—"

"Don't you dare, pretty girl. Do not dare to utter the name that has been carefully hidden for centuries. You would not even know what it was, were it not for your trusting sister. I have no relationship with you. I will not hesitate to terminate your ability to speak before I will allow you to call forth such evil."

Inezia left her place next to CeCe. Her words were clear and her stance was ready. Tremble could see that the woman would have no hesitation in performing magic on Belladonna.

"The Evil with which you were united in marriage. The Evil from whom you produced a child—a devil from another world." Belladonna's words were sharp. From the look on Inezia's face, their aim had been precise.

"Sister! Silence! Enough! Our emotions are running high, but I shall not stand by and allow you to attack Inezia. We must concentrate our efforts on solving current problems."

"You must concentrate your efforts. I believe that I shall go and visit my dear Laken and see what you all have done to him."

Before anyone could react, Belladonna was gone in a puff of smoke.

Chapter Four

"SHE'S ALWAYS HAD quite the temper. Her bark is worse than her bite. After she calms down, things will be better." Jasmine paused for a moment. "I hope."

Tremble watched as her mother walked toward the door where Belladonna had previously entered. Jasmine put a spell on the area.

"Did you expect Belladonna to be so hostile? I imagined that she would have been happier to see you?"

"Tremble, I love my sister. We have a strong bond. There has always been a rivalry, though. I suppose that is natural. She resents that I am the firstborn and was heir to the throne. I would have gladly given the role to her." Jasmine walked around the room near the walls. Tremble was amazed to see that as Jasmine walked past a wall, the colors changed. "The last twenty-one years have been hard on her. She felt that she had to put her life on hold. Belladonna should be married with her own family by now."

"Why do you think that she has not married? She must have had opportunities." Tremble watched as Jasmine walked in circles. It was beginning to make her dizzy.

"Belladonna has had suitors from many of the neighboring kingdoms. She has not moved forward because her heart still belongs to Xavier. Her hostility, in some part, toward me is because of the role I played in his death. She knows that it was never my intent in any way for that to happen. It does not help, though, that it was his love for me that caused him to attack Forrest. Heaven help me, I did not know. I do not think that Forrest had any idea that Xavier would react in that manner to his proposal to me. Forrest would have not done that in front of him."

"Yes, he would have." Inezia had been silent up until that point.

"Why do you say that?"

"Oh, my dear, I say that because it is in Forrest's very nature to be a fighter. You seem to forget that my powers give me a bird's eye view to many things." Inezia paused and appeared to be listening for something. "Forrest certainly did not want any harm physically to come to Xavier. I am sure though that he wanted Xavier to view his proposal. He wanted it to be clear who had your heart. If Xavier could have looked past his anger, he might have seen that he also had feelings for Belladonna. He revealed this in many of his actions, yet, I think he was too blind to realize it himself. Each time he would show her affection, Belladonna developed a little more hope. Then, you would come back from some journey you had been on and his affections would swing back to you."

"This makes my heart so sad. I would have done anything to prevent my sister's heartache. I was just young and naïve and only concerned about Forrest's attentions." Jasmine stopped walking and stood in front of Tremble. "Enough of this. We do not have time to worry about Belladonna at this point. We need to concentrate on making a plan to find Forrest. I must admit that despite the incredible danger, I am thrilled at the thought of seeing my beloved husband."

Tremble watched as momentarily the worry and concern left Jasmine's face and was replaced by happiness and joy. She thought about what a special time it would be for her parents to be reunited after so many years and for the three of them to be together for the very first time.

"How will we even begin to find him?" Tremble rose and started to pace as Jasmine had a few minutes earlier.

"Tremble, there are many things that we did not have time to teach you in our few weeks of your training."

CeCe rose from where she had been sitting. Tremble was somewhat amazed at the show of emotion that she had made over the news about Laken. CeCe had succeeded in hiding her emotional side up until that point. She appeared to have regained her composure.

"There's one aspect of your magical abilities that you need no training. Concentration and guidance is all you need."

"What's that? I am all for not having to learn more spells."

"Your powers of detection are vast and resourceful. Even Dana and Andrew recognized this as you were growing up."

"I could find keys and the remote control. That doesn't mean that I can find a person who is being held captive."

"Oh, but it did. We talked about this the other day. You remember that little girl."

"Yes. It's not the same thing though."

"Is it not? That sweet little girl was being held by someone who had power over her. How is that different than the situation Forrest is in now?"

Tremble's pacing increased in intensity. CeCe's words caused her mind to race in a thousand directions and a feeling of fear returned to the pit of her stomach.

"You aren't telling the end of that story, CeCe. Mom reminded us that it didn't end so well, remember?"

"Indeed, I do remember. It's why we put a block on that memory. We did not want you to carry that feeling of remorse around with you. It was beyond your control." CeCe caught up with Tremble's pacing and stopped her. "This is different. We know that Forrest is alive. We also know that the being that holds him captive wants very much for you to find him."

"CeCe's words are true, Tremble." Jasmine joined them. "We have come to the point that we can no longer run. You are the fulfillment of the prophecy. It is you who Scordato wishes to challenge. Forrest and I were merely stand-ins until the real thing could grow up."

"There are many things about this story that do not make sense to me. I need a clearer understanding before we go forward." Jasmine and CeCe nodded. "I understand that I was hidden in the mortal world for my protection. We now know that Scordato or one of his clones was in close proximity to me on many occasions. You say that he wants to do battle with me as a grown opponent. Then, why is everything cloaked in secrecy?"

Jasmine walked away from Tremble. CeCe bowed her head and sat down. It was Inezia who began to speak.

"Tremble, a mother's greatest fear is losing her child. Thankfully, the universe sees fit, for the most part, to make that an uncommon occurrence. In every world, there are such women who face their greatest fear head-on and must live with the outcome for the rest of their lives. I loved the children of Marcellus and Claudia. I loved them as my own because, as you now know, I am one of those women. I have loved every generation of children who have come forth from my two dearest friends. I may have loved this dear girl here most of all."

Jasmine turned toward Inezia. Tremble could see tears in her eyes.

"The family, close and extended, punished Jasmine and Forrest for falling in love. They were loved and they were hated by their own flesh and blood. It was fear that drove those feelings. It is fear that taints all of our lives. The prophecy has hung over this family for generations. It was a fear among those who served as well. It caused division."

"I was not just afraid of Scordato." Jasmine walked to Inezia and took hold of the old woman's hand. "When I placed you in the care of Dana and Andrew, he was my primary concern. He was my long-term concern. I didn't know then that he was being influenced by a power far worse than he would ever be. But, in the short term, we were equally worried about what the extended family or even the other citizens of Neverwrong might do."

"You mean the protectors, like CeCe?" Tremble's eyes followed the expressions on each woman's face. There was much emotion in them.

"For the most part, those who have worked for the Royal Family have been loyal and diligent in their work. There are many of them and they are assigned to different branches of the family. Their loyalty was not only to those who descended from Perpetua or Baldric." Jasmine looked at CeCe. "Those who have protected the line of Perpetua have always been the best."

"Tremble, for many of us who have worked as guardians, it has been a family business, so to speak. Our parents and grandparents did this work for one line of the family. Those who have worked for the families of the other sisters have their loyal protectors as well. We told you about how close the original sisters were. That was very true. The generation after them could also be described that way. In the years since, things have changed." Tremble sensed that CeCe's words were not telling the whole story.

"I would never have chosen to be the Supreme Ruler of Neverwrong. Neither would have Forrest. It was our legacy, our destiny. We honored our role in this world." Jasmine took in a deep breath. "You have seen some of the jealousy of my own sister. We want what we cannot have, I suppose. She wanted my life. I would have been content with hers. Our cousins, generations far removed, looked at Forrest and me as some celebrity couple, to use a mortal term. They also saw our union and our child as a threat to their lives."

"You can only avoid the inevitable for so long, Tremble." Inezia's words seemed to have a double meaning. "The prophecy has to be fulfilled. It is destined to happen. One of the most horrid things about this chain of events is that there are those who think they can stop it."

"Stop it? I don't understand." Tremble furrowed her brow and looked at each of them.

"There are those who thought that if you did not exist there would not be a prophecy any longer." CeCe did not hesitate with her answer. "Your guardians were trained to protect you from anything and everything, not just Scordato. We did not tell your mortal parents that the threat was greater than just him."

"After some time passed and Jasmine found her way to me, we began to study all that we knew of Amadeus, Scordato, and this wretched prophecy." Inezia's words were forceful. "I told

Jasmine what The Evil behind Scordato was. We began to understand that Scordato was merely a pawn. He had his own agenda though, and that was to show his power and to take back what he thought was his legacy."

"The Supreme Rulership of Neverwrong?" Slowly, the pieces of the story were taking shape in Tremble's mind.

"Yes. What he failed to understand, or perhaps accept, is that it was never his to begin with."

"What? He was the firstborn of Marcellus and Claudia. Didn't that give him the—"

"He was the first child of the Supreme *Enchanter* Marcellus and Her Royal Highness Claudia. Neither of them ever set foot in Neverwrong. The Kingdom of Neverwrong was created by The Seven after they came down from the mountain. It has never been ruled by Marcellus' and Claudia's firstborn or even the second born, for that matter. Perpetua was the first Supreme Ruler of Neverwrong and the firstborns from her line have succeeded her." Inezia nodded her head and continued. "For all the wisdom he has gained in his study of the magical world, The Evil that controls him does not allow him to see this one fact."

"So, even if he kills me, he cannot take control."

"No, he cannot." Jasmine's answer was firm. "He could kill everyone in the Royal Family and still not accomplish that."

"But? There's a 'but' in there somewhere."

"That's right, smart girl." Inezia's smile was broad. "In Scordato's rage, he would probably try to do that. Kill off the entire Royal Family. That would indeed make The Evil that I once called my husband happy."

"Why?"

"Because then, everything that belonged to Marcellus and Claudia would be gone. That is what *he* really wants."

"Again, I have got to ask—why?"

"Because The Evil, who we carefully call Sebastian, asked Marcellus to bestow magical powers on him. Marcellus refused. He refused to give him even a little of what he desired most."

"I still don't understand."

"Oh, my dear, to truly understand you would have to have been there. It is like every story that involves beings who have emotions. Sebastian came to our world seeking something he could not have on his own. He infiltrated our lives and tried to maneuver us into giving him what he wanted. With some of us, he succeeded. But, not with Marcellus, who was stern and stubborn. Baldric is very much like his father. He could be Sebastian's friend. He refused to give him powers. He thought that Sebastian was from a world that had deemed themselves unworthy. Marcellus could not see past that."

Inezia rested for a moment. The weight of the story seemed heavy. It tired her to speak it.

"This is what fueled Sebastian's wrath. It became his goal to destroy everything that belonged to Marcellus. I do not know precisely what state Marcellus and Claudia are in. After I saw the curse that Scordato put on his own brother and sisters, I knew where the idea had come from." Inezia put her head in her hands. "Scordato's heart would not allow him to carry out the curse to the extent that Sebastian had done. He could confine his siblings. He could not render them completely helpless without interaction. I fear that those statues of Marcellus and Claudia are a literal and figurative representation of what Sebastian wanted for Marcellus. He wanted them to be helpless, frozen. He left the rest of our family in our original kingdom frozen in time. He had to do something worse to Marcellus."

"Somehow, I think you are trying to tell me something. Why

don't you just say it?" The feeling of fear within Tremble was now taking on an edge of anxiousness.

"Tremble, perhaps it would be best if you tell us what you have deduced from all you have been told." CeCe's roundabout response was not what Tremble wanted to hear.

"I have to live the prophecy, fulfill the prophecy, but also figure out the backstory? There's nothing fair about this, ladies."

"You hit the nail on the head." CeCe smiled, but Tremble could tell that it was a momentary emotion. "There's nothing fair about any of this."

"Scordato is a puppet and Sebastian is pulling the strings, is that correct?"

"Precisely." Inezia shook her head. "Sebastian controls everything."

"Is he the reason that you do not trust some of your Royal cousins?"

"Not directly; I am not sure that we can blame him for their jealously and fear." Jasmine resumed pacing. "Some do not like that the kingdom rulership has stayed with only one branch of the family. I understand that. Some are fearful that the prophecy being fulfilled will destroy our world as we know it. I understand that fear as well."

"Especially if the heir fulfills the prophecy as it is written and turns her back on her homeland."

"Yes, there's that. Or the fear that the heir does not have the power to defeat the oppressor."

"And, they really don't even know who the oppressor is, do they?"

"No, they don't, my daughter. It is a secret that has been more carefully hidden than where you have been all these years."

"Why does Sebastian care about me?"

"Tremble, we have tried to carefully tell you that you possess great power." CeCe began to answer her question.

"Yes, I have descended from two of the most powerful enchanters ever. You have told me that repeatedly."

"Indeed. What we haven't told you is what that really means. Jasmine, I think you better take this one. Tremble, I think you better sit down."

Tremble obeyed sitting on the bench.

"My daughter, I had hoped that your father might be with us when you learned this truth. I could use Forrest's strength right now." Jasmine paused and took a deep breath.

"I am here, my love."

Tremble fell off the bench she was sitting on. The others were visibly shaken as well. The voice was distinctive. It was the one Tremble had heard weeks earlier in her dream.

"Be careful. I am telling this to Tremble now so that we can find you."

There was silence. Tremble found herself looking up at the ceiling as if Forrest was going to swoop down. She shook her head.

"Tremble, the Letters of Perpetua are full of great wisdom. I would not say that they are a prophecy, for they really do not foretell any events. Yet, they do give us a little inkling of some things that might happen. One of the things that she talks about in one of her last letters is the Child of Power. She talks about a child that will be born who shall have the *greatest* power that an enchanter has ever had. Please listen to me closely. Not the greatest power that anyone of the Royal Family has ever had. This child would have the greatest power that any enchanter in any kingdom or world has ever had."

Tremble could feel the moisture leaving her mouth. Her

hands began to tingle. Her vision began to blur.

"Stay with us, Tremble." CeCe's voice and a burst of cold air brought Tremble back from the fog she was travelling into.

"I knew this information would be overwhelming. I do not know how to lessen this news. It is way too much for your young mind to have to process. You must, however, have this knowledge in order to know how to move forward."

Jasmine looked at CeCe and Inezia. Both women had serious expressions as they nodded in encouragement. Tremble thought she heard the whisper of another voice, a deeper one. She could not make out the words.

"Perpetua told us in her letters that the Child of Power would descend from Supreme Enchanter Marcellus and Her Royal Highness Claudia. We do not think that she totally came up with this idea on her own. We believe that she was guided by the words of another great enchanter. Inezia has probably not told you that the land they came from was the most magical world in all of history. It was also one of the most peaceful. The magic was clean. It was only used for good. This is why Claudia's powers of healing were so mighty and why healers have been such an important part of our family."

"I understand that you are trying to tell me that I may be the Child of Power. Is that correct?" Tremble's voice was barely above a whisper.

"Yes, my dear one. It is a grave responsibility and a grand opportunity."

"How do you know that it is me?"

"There are several things in her letters that elude to it being you. The Child of Power would be the firstborn. The child would be from two lines of the original family. The child would come from a world created just for it."

Tremble's whole body began to shake with a level of fear unlike any she had ever experienced before.

"I don't know what to say, except that I am terrified." Tremble's voice cracked as she said the last word. "I know I have to do this. I just don't understand how I can have so much power when I have seen so little of it thus far."

Jasmine knelt down in front of her daughter. She grasped both of Tremble's forearms near the elbows and gave them a tight squeeze.

"This is another reason why we need to get to your father and get him out of the grasp of Scordato. The two of us together, with Inezia and CeCe's help, can unleash this power that is smoldering within you."

"I cannot do this without Laken."

Tremble did not know where the thought came from. It was out of her mouth before she realized what she was saying. She was convinced that it was the truth.

"Tremble, I do not know if that is possible. Regardless, I think that we need your father to help us. There is no doubt that he and I have a strong bond. Even yet, I am not sure how we shall begin to locate him. Scordato has a tight shield around his location."

"Scordato wants to face me. He knows that I will be looking for my parents. We cannot be sure if he knows I have found you or not. I may be crazy, but I think I know someone who can help us find Scordato."

"Who would that be?"

"An old friend from home. A friend who is trained to meet an enemy head on."

"A mortal? Oh, Tremble, I don't think that is a good idea." Jasmine rose and looked at the others. "Involving a mortal will only cause another level of problems. How could this human possibly find Forrest?"

"He has the power of love."

"Love for who?"

Tremble looked past Jasmine's questioning expression and made eye contact with CeCe. This woman, who had up until recently been her professional mentor and a stranger outside of that, shook her head and closed her eyes. Tremble paused and waited for her reaction. As she opened her eyes again, she gave Tremble a smile that could only be described as resolution.

"Okay, Tremble, we can try this. I don't know what will happen. We can try."

"What is going on here? Who are you two talking about?"

"Jasmine, have you ever heard of the Man of Steel?"

Chapter Five

"YES, MOM. I'M FINE."

Tremble smiled and waved as Dana began to chatter rapidly. She realized that it had been too long since she had checked in with her mother. So much had happened in a short time.

"It's been incredible being with Jasmine. We are visiting friends of hers. The scene is right out of a Disney movie. I'm a princess in a tower."

"Oh, Tremble, stop making jokes. You think that this re-assures me. It really makes me think you are hiding something from me."

Talking through a magical tablet and being literally a world away did not stop Dana from sounding like Tremble's mother.

"Really, Mom. I'm in the tower of a castle."

"Tremble, please stop being descriptive." Bridget appeared over Dana's shoulder.

"Sorry. Mom, I need for you to contact Sylvia and see if you can find out where her son is working now." Tremble chose her words carefully.

"What? Why do you need to know where J—"

Tremble could see that Bridget jabbed Dana in the arm as she was about to say Jake's name.

"Ah, you know her son works out of town these days."

Tremble wished that she was videoing her mother's facial expressions as the woman tried to figure out what was going on as well as how to not reveal too much information.

"Yes, he travels with his job now. Sometimes he is out of the country."

"Yes, I remember. I hope that his mother keeps up with him."

"Tremble, we don't really need to contact his mother in order to find him." Bridget's face came on the screen. "Is CeCe there?"

"Yes, Bridget. You know who to contact. It shouldn't be hard to find out. Tremble feels very certain about this. All we can do is believe in her."

"Right. Have you thought about transport?"

"He is aware of the circumstances. I believe he should willingly accept the assignment. It would probably be best for you to take Dana with you when you meet him. That should overcome any matters of trust on his part."

Tremble could not help but think that the conversation sounded like something out of an espionage movie. With the knowledge that she now had on the work that CeCe and Bridget had been doing for decades, Tremble imagined that they had all of the equipment and resources at their disposal that James Bond might have.

"Do you suggest a direct flight after that?"

"Precisely. It might be good to involve Edgar. I do not want you to leave Dana at this point."

"Why can't Dana come, too? Dana likes to take trips."

Tremble heard her mother talking about herself before she grabbed the tablet and put her face in the conversation.

"Mom, I don't think that's such a good—"

"Dana, I thoroughly understand why you would like to be here."

Jasmine took the tablet away from CeCe and changed it to large screen view. Bridget followed her lead and did the same on her side.

"We do not, at this present point, have a good place for you to be hidden. It would be very complicated for us to try and take you with us on this next phase of the journey."

"What about with your sister? Surely, she has space."

"Yes, my sister. Space is not a problem. She is not the welcoming sort at this present time."

"I don't understand."

"Bridget will explain it to you later." CeCe walked in front of Jasmine. "Bridget, let me know as soon as you are able to make contact with Tremble's friend. I would imagine that we should be able to arrange transport in just a few hours."

"Yes, I agree. I will be in touch."

"Mom, it sounds like we need to end this call now. Please, don't worry. I am fine. Jasmine is taking good care of me. It may be hard for me to communicate with you while we, ah, travel. I will send you a postcard."

"Postcard?"

Dana came back into view. As Tremble stood on her side of the image, it made them look as if they were standing in front of each other, instead of a world apart. Tremble longed to reach out physically to her. Taking a deep breath, she fought back the emotion that was mounting inside her.

"You know he will help take care of me." Tremble whispered as she gave her mother a hopeful smile.

"I know he will. I have no doubt that Bridget will find him and that he will not hesitate to come to your aid." Dana paused and bit her lower lip. "I wish I could come, too. I don't have any superpowers to offer."

"You have more powers than anyone." Tremble gave her mother a big thumbs up. "Mom, before you go, will you do one thing for me?"

"Anything."

"Could you hold Choo Choo up and let me talk to her?"

Tremble watched as her mother left her view for a moment. She could hear Dana calling the little dog. A few minutes later, Dana came back into view with the light-haired toy poodle in her arms.

"Oh, Choo Choo, I miss you." Tremble could see that the dog was wagging its tail and looking around, following her voice. "She can't see me on the screen, can she?"

"It doesn't appear so."

"Scratch her behind the ears. Give her kisses. I love you, Choo. You take care of Mom for me."

Choo Choo kept wagging her tail. The animal was obviously confused by hearing Tremble's voice and not seeing her. It made a lump form in Tremble's throat as she looked at her precious pet in her mother's arms. She wondered if she would ever snuggle with either one of them again.

"Bridget, we will talk later. Dana, chin up. We are making progress. We are signing off now."

CeCe did not give Tremble a chance to say anything else.

She stared at the blank screen of the tablet. CeCe had turned it off. She could not even see the friendly fluttering wings of the butterfly image.

"This is not getting any easier."

Tremble did not look up at anyone as she said the words. She knew that she must gather strength within herself to find the courage she was about to need.

"I feel guilty that we have not been telling Mom everything. I can't imagine that many of the truths you have revealed to me over the last few hours would ease her mind."

"I realize that this is probably a time in your life that you need Dana more than ever." Jasmine came up and stood behind Tremble. She began to softly stroke her hair. "I know that I am a poor substitute, but I would love to offer you some of that motherly support."

The words had been on the tip of her tongue for hours. Tremble was surprised when the thought first occurred to her. It seemed like a betrayal of sorts. She knew that wasn't an accurate assumption. The circumstances had long ago made it the right thing; she just did not know it.

"I would like that. I think I would also like to call you something other than Jasmine. Mom does not seem quite right yet. It's a little too personal. How about I start with Mother?"

Tremble did not turn around to see Jasmine's face. It was not necessary. Tremble could see the bright glimmer of Jasmine's aura as it flashed beautifully soft, yet intense, colors. It reminded her of a laser light show.

"I would love that." Jasmine's voice quivered.

Tremble rose and faced the woman who had given her life. Then Jasmine had given up her own life in sacrifice for her child. Tremble saw a pool of tears glistening in the sapphire blue of her mother's eyes. She realized that for the first time, Tremble had been able to give something back.

THE EVENING TURNED into night. Inezia magically prepared a lovely dinner for them. It was as though they were all starving but not hungry. Living in a world of enchantment now, Tremble slowly became accustomed to whatever they needed 'appearing' almost by the sheer wishing for it. After the meal, beds materialized within the tower room. The beds hovered a few feet off the ground. The mattresses were plush and comfortable. The pillows were soft. The most luxurious material Tremble had ever felt adorned the beds as coverings. Layers and layers of sheets and blankets combined providing the right temperature to sleep within.

Everyone became quiet in their own thoughts as they settled into their individual nests of comfort. Each had a view of the stars via a different window. Tremble could see a pink moon with a small cluster of stars near it.

"Is this the same night sky that I saw in the mortal world?" Tremble whispered her question hoping it would only be heard by those who were still awake.

"It is, my dear." Jasmine's soft voice whispered back. "It only looks different because that is the way Marcellus wished it to be."

"So, my Mom, Dana, is looking at the same sky."

"She is indeed. I understand how she feels tonight as I looked at the moon and wished for you thousands of nights myself. Send her some special thoughts of love."

"I will." Tremble paused for a moment as she concentrated on a thought of love for Dana. "I wish I had known about you on some of those nights, Mother. I would have sent *you* some love."

There was silence after Tremble's comment. Within her mind, she heard Jasmine's voice with an emotional 'thank you.'

"CeCe left an hour ago to meet Edgar."

Tremble stretched and yawned as her eyes opened. A bright Neverwrong morning shone through all of the windows.

"Who's Edgar?"

"Edgar is one of our most trusted protectors. He's also Bridget's brother."

Jasmine sat in front of a dressing table that had appeared in the room. She was brushing her ebony hair with long strokes. Inezia came out of the bathroom. It was another room that Jasmine had created within the tower as the need arose.

"Edgar is the spitting image of his grandfather." Inezia had on a deep mauve colored dress with several pockets and buttons. It looked more functional than stylish.

"Neverwrong is quite the family affair, isn't it?"

"Well, Tremble, our world has been a close knit family for generations. We trust those who have been loyal to us."

Jasmine rose from the dressing table. She was wearing a beautiful pale blue jumpsuit, similar to one that Tremble had seen Belladonna wear. As she walked toward Tremble's bed, a deep lavender one in the same style appeared in her hand.

"Do you like it?"

"Oh, it is beautiful. I was hoping that we wouldn't be wearing dresses every day. Cramps the style of a crime fighter."

"Crime fighter?" Inezia asked her question as she was creating a beautiful table of breakfast in the center of the room.

"I'm sorry, Inezia. It's another Hollywood thing. Mother, please tell me what Edgar is doing."

The three of them sat down at the breakfast table. Tremble still had on her silky pajamas and bedhead hair. There was something about the morning that gave her renewed hope and that translated into a ravenous appetite.

"Edgar accompanied Bridget and Dana as they went to find Jake. They were successful. Edgar is escorting your fearless friend to CeCe. They will get along splendidly. Edgar is a high ranking member of the Neverwrong Army. He was also Forrest's right-hand man in his laboratory."

"Why haven't I heard of him before?"

Tremble picked up a small bowl of chopped fruit that was in the center of her plate. Some of the pieces looked familiar. Others did not. The colors were beautiful. She could already taste the variety of sweet flavors.

"There are many players in this story. I'm sure that Laken, CeCe, and Bridget have only hit the highlights of those who have been involved."

The mention of Laken caused Tremble to stop for a moment. Her heart pained to think of him all alone in the Garden of Stone. It was her strongest desire to free him from his stone-like state. It amazed her that this was now forefront to her, an even greater desire than to rid the world of Scordato or Sebastian.

"Edgar and Jake will have plenty to talk about on the flight. It was thought that it would be best to use the more conventional means of transport from the mortal world to here. The change in atmosphere is enough of a shock on a mortal body without the speed of travel that you experience."

"I can't believe that Jake is coming. It's all so surreal." Tremble selected a piece of breakfast bread from a basket in front of her. She could smell something akin to lavender as one of its ingredients.

"You doubted that he would be willing to help you?"

Inezia passed her a large pitcher that contained a beautiful liquid beverage. The color almost matched the outfit that Jasmine was wearing. Tremble searched her mind for what possible fruit it could be made from

"It is giggleberry juice, my dear." Inezia smiled as Tremble poured a glass of it. "It is one of our most delightful fruits. Each piece has a different face on it."

The thought of eating a fruit with a face did not appeal to Tremble. She did, however, try a sip of the beverage. Before she realized what was happening, she was giggling.

"You were just dying to try that on her, naughty Inezia." Jasmine smiled as she took a drink of the beverage. "After you have drunk it a few times, the giggle reaction wears off."

"We are not all gloom and doom, my dear." Inezia filled up Tremble's glass. "We like to have fun, too."

"I knew that Jake would be willing to help me." Tremble went back to the question Inezia had asked. "I am just surprised that he was able to be retrieved from his Navy assignment so quickly."

"Oh, my dear, you have not come to fully understand the power of magic. We can make anything happen in the mortal world that we wish to occur."

"Anything?" Tremble gave her mother a non-believing look.

"Yes. That does not mean that we will. We do not like to interfere with the nature of things. We do not like to rewrite history, so to speak. But, we could, it is within our powers."

"What Jasmine is trying to say is that extracting one mortal is not that hard of a task, as long as he is willing to come."

"He and CeCe will be here shortly. Is there anything that we need to know about him?"

"Well, he is very strong and athletic. He has a frightful stubborn streak. And, he is not overly happy with the magical world."

"What? I do not understand. He could only have a little knowledge of it."

"Oh, he has quite a bit of knowledge as it relates to how he was influenced by magic to leave his high school sweetheart and suddenly join the Navy. That is something that he didn't like."

"Laken did that." Jasmine took a deep breath and shook her head. "He was trained to protect you from anyone he thought might be a threat. As you have learned, that was more than Scordato. We knew that there might even be members of the Royals who might try to infiltrate your life. It is not an excuse by any means."

"I realize all of that now. Keep in mind though that Jake doesn't have this knowledge. All he knows is that someone messed with him and took his girl away."

"Does he know that it was Laken?"

Tremble thought about Jasmine's question. Her mind raced backwards to the conversation that she and Jake had the night of her birthday in his car. She did not remember saying who had been involved.

"I don't think he does. I think that I just told him that he had been magically influenced to join the Navy."

"That is good." Jasmine rose from the table. "He might not be willing to assist us if he knew that it could help the one who influenced him."

"I really do not think that would matter to Jake. He would

help someone regardless of what had been done to him."

"He sounds like a good man. I look forward to meeting him."

All three of them had finished breakfast. With a flick of her wrist the breakfast table and their beds disappeared. Tremble was left in the center of the room holding her jumpsuit.

"Young lady, I suggest that you get ready." Inezia pointed to the door of the bathroom. It instantly opened. "That young man will be in our world shortly. We shall rendezvous with CeCe at the Garden of Stone."

"Why there?" Tremble walked toward the open door.

"Because it is always best to start at the beginning, and so much of what we face today and into the future, begins with those who are presently stationed there."

As Tremble entered the bathroom and closed the door, she could not help but think about the three who were suspended in a state of stone. Looking at herself in the reflection of the mirror, she said out loud what was in her heart.

"If a Child of Power I indeed am, I do so wish that this power can be used to bring back those who have been lost. It seems that no matter what anyone else may fear, leaving them that way would be the worst fulfillment to any prophecy."

Chapter Six

"**P**ACING WILL NOT make them arrive any sooner." Shortly after Tremble dressed, Jasmine instantly transported them back to the Garden of Stone. Tremble had taken a few minutes to quietly visit with Laken before she had begun pacing in the middle of the garden.

"This apple must not have fallen far from that tree." Tremble pointed to Jasmine. "You just about made a path in the floor of the tower room with your pacing yesterday."

"Point taken. I have traveled thousands of miles with my pacing through the years."

"Tremble."

Even though she was expecting it, the voice caught her off guard. It was like the sound of home to her. Slowly, she turned around and saw that the face matched the voice. The look of concern on the handsome face was quickly replaced by a smile as Tremble began running to meet him.

"You came."

The only words she spoke came in a whisper in Jake's ear as he picked her up off the ground.

"Of course, I did."

His breath in her ear as he whispered a reply reminded her of a hundred times he had done so before. It felt so secure. Her heart skipped a beat as she felt his arms tighten around her.

"Maybe if I close my eyes and wish really hard, this will all be a dream."

"I have briefed Jake regarding our situation here." CeCe interrupted their conversation.

Jake wasn't taking the hint so Tremble had to nudge him to put her back on the ground. She wasn't quite ready to get down to business.

"You saw my mom. Is she okay?"

"Yes, she seemed fine. Worried, but fine. She barely stopped hugging me the whole time we were together. She held my hand while we travelled, if that's what you call it."

Tremble turned to look at CeCe.

"Time was of the essence. Bridget, Edgar, and Dana travelled to where Jake was stationed the fastest way possible."

"So, my mother has now travelled magically?"

"It wasn't the first time. We travelled that way once when you were a child. It was an emergency. Don't be distressed. She is fine. Bridget and Dana are staying in New York for a few days."

"Why?"

"Because that is where Jake and Edgar flew out of on Neverwrong Airlines. We think it is better that they do not return to your home for a while. It's a diversion."

"Where then is Choo Choo?"

"She's staying with VeVette and her family."

"Oh, brother. So where am I then?"

"You are with your mother in New York. Your mother had a conference to attend. Dana said that VeVette was very good with Choo Choo."

"Good grief, yes. Let's just hope that VeVe doesn't talk to anyone at Kaleidoscope."

"Why is that?"

"Because, I am supposed to be taking care of my mother who had to have surgery, remember? You have woven a story that even you can't keep up with."

"This does not concern us. We can fix it later."

"I endeavored to explain the Garden of Stone to Jake while we were travelling, but I believe seeing it will be the best explanation."

They walked through a clearing and back to where three stone statues now stood. Jake's expression didn't change much when he saw the statues.

"The two that you see standing here, side by side, are the Supreme Enchanter Marcellus and his wife, Her Royal Highness Claudia. These two are Tremble's ancestors, her grandparents from several generations previous."

"Is there a reason why these statues were made with such pained expressions? It's not a very flattering look for either one of them."

Everyone was silent after Jake's statement. He continued to walk around the statues before turning back to face Tremble.

"Did I say something wrong?"

"Jake, these aren't statues. They are actually Marcellus and Claudia." Tremble saw a puzzled look come over Jake's face, and he shook his head indicating that he didn't understand. "They were turned to stone in this very spot a couple hundred years ago."

"Her words are true, young man." Inezia walked toward Jake. "I was not here when it happened. I am, however, very acquainted with The Evil that did this to them. My dear sweet Claudia and Marcellus are within that stone. We have reason to believe that this put them in a suspended state. They can probably see us and hear us."

"No way."

Jake looked from Inezia to Tremble to CeCe. Everyone was shaking their heads affirmatively.

"And, what about this guy over here?" Jake walked to Laken. "Is he the same way, too?"

No one said a word. Jake turned back to the group and looked from face to face. His brow furrowed as he got to Tremble's.

"What's the matter? Did you know him? This isn't your father?" Jake turned to CeCe. "You told me that I was going to help Tremble find her father."

"He's not my father, Jake." Tremble wiped the tears from her eyes. "I know him. This is Laken. He's my Protector."

"I've heard that name. You mentioned him the night you told me about all this magic stuff." Jake ran his fingers through his missing hair. "He was like your bodyguard or something. What happened? Why is he like this?"

"It's a long story, Jake. Longer than we probably have time for right now. The short version is that he is my Protector and he is my friend. He got this way trying to help me. I've got to do something to try and get him out of this state."

"Isn't he—"

"Don't say it. No, he's not." Tremble's voice grew strong as she was speaking. "We are going to find my father. He has a pendant like the one I am wearing." Tremble showed Jake the pendant that hung around her neck. "It's also like the one around Laken's neck."

Jake walked back to Laken and looked at the pendant.

"It's not stone. Is that a good sign?"

"I think it is. It's one of the reasons that I think I can help him. Maybe I can help my grandparents, too. I don't know. I've got to try."

"So all of you think that these statue people can hear us and see us?" Jake watched as they all shook their heads agreeing. "Okay, then." Jake walked to the front of Laken. "You protected Tremble. You devoted a lot of time to that if I remember the story correctly. That makes you important to Tremble and important to me. However, I have my suspicions that you are the one who made me join the Navy."

Tremble couldn't conceal the gasp that came out of her. Jasmine reached over and squeezed her hand.

"My suspicions were just confirmed. I don't like what you did. There's no doubt about that. The kid I used to be would probably use you as a punching bag. That was then. The man I am now understands that you had a job to do—protect Tremble. That's a mighty important one. You had to do what you thought was right. You had to protect. Now, I'm going to help her get you back to your natural state. Then, we are going to have a long talk."

Tremble closed her eyes and squeezed Jasmine's hand. She thought to herself that her Mom would never believe what just happened. She had to hold tight to that memory and share it with her.

"Okay." Jake turned and faced them. He winked at Tremble. "Magical people, let's get this show on the road. What's the first step to finding Tremble's father?"

"Well, Jake, we think that Tremble herself is the first step. We believe that Tremble has some incredible powers of discovery, to find things."

"Oh, yeah, that's no secret. She found my class ring twice in Taylor's Lake. She can find anything."

"More examples of your ability to find things, Tremble. You keep denying this skill, yet everyone in your life seems to know you have it." CeCe gave Tremble a questioning look.

"Okay, CeCe. How are we supposed to begin? I've never been in the same room with Forrest. How am I going to be able to detect him?"

"Through Jasmine. You are genetically connected to both of them. Jasmine is emotionally connected, bonded, to Forrest. I think that through Jasmine, you will be able to pick up where Forrest is."

"Tremble, CeCe is right." Inezia joined the discussion. "Immortal bonds are even stronger than mortal ones. Add the strength of your parents' magical abilities to that and you have a very powerful signal. It is a signal that their daughter, the Child of Power, should be able to receive."

"What's this 'Child of Power' thing?" Jake looked at Tremble.

"It is another long story, young man. The short version is that Tremble is believed to be the most powerful enchanter ever to have lived."

"What?" Jake's eyes got big as he looked at Tremble. "Wow! I wasted my time being afraid of your parents. You are the one who could have straightened me out if I got out of line."

"Oh, shut up. This whole power child thing is news to me, too. Quite frankly, I don't know if I believe it."

"Perpetua knew of what she spoke." Inezia's spoke with certainty. "You must have the confidence to rise to this."

"Regardless, the first thing we have got to do is find Forrest. Inezia, I trust your wisdom in this regard. Is there a physical location that you think Jasmine and I should begin this process?"

Inezia seemed caught off guard by Tremble's question. She walked over to a stone bench that was near a large tree. She sat down with her back to the tree.

As Tremble waited for the woman to begin speaking, she looked up into the tree. At first, she thought that her eyes were playing tricks on her as it appeared that the leaves had faces. Tremble rubbed her eyes and looked back again. The leaves were smiling at her.

"Those leaves above Inezia's head, do they look a little strange to you?"

"Oh, do not be alarmed, Tremble." Jasmine began to answer. "That is a face tree. It was the creation of Claudia's, specifically for this garden. It is ironic because these leaves have watched over her for hundreds of years now."

"Inezia, what does this mean? You surely must understand it better than anyone."

Tremble walked toward it. She felt the shadow of Jake right behind her.

"I thought that I had seen some weird stuff in the military."

Jake shook his head as he looked at some of the taller branches. Tremble thought she saw one of the leaves wink at him and another one spit something.

"Do these leaves spit?"

"Yes, my dear, these leaves can do many things. I have seen their reactions to quite a few of the Royals who have visited here. They are an excellent judge of character. The spitting has to do with discontent on their part." Inezia watched Jake. "This young man here is getting closer to some of the leaves than they like. If the spit reaches his skin, he will learn not to stand so close in the future." Jake suddenly backed away. The action caused Inezia to heartedly laugh. "I assure you, it is not poison. You would feel quite a sting though."

"I have heard stories of the screeching of the tree in this garden. Is this what they are referring to?" CeCe joined Jake in his investigation.

"Indeed. The tree will make quite a ruckus if someone threatening ventures near Claudia."

"That should be a way to tell if Scordato is around." Tremble sat down next to Inezia on the bench.

"Actually, that is not correct."

"Why? Isn't he one of the most threatening beings in Neverwrong?"

"He is not threatening to Claudia or Marcellus for that matter."

"Why not?"

"He is their son."

The group was silent as they pondered Inezia's answer. Scordato was Amadeus. Amadeus was Claudia's and Marcellus' young son, their firstborn. He would not be a threat to them.

"This tree has great perception. It cannot, however, see past its own place." Inezia took hold of Tremble's hand. "You asked me how we begin the process of you and Jasmine finding Forrest. I think we should begin where Jasmine's and Forrest's love for each other was sealed."

"In the courtyard where they were married?"

"No, that was merely a ceremony; their love was sealed when Forrest declared his love in the Garden of Mystery. You have been told that what occurs within this garden is permanent, unyielding. This is one of the reasons that Forrest chose the location for his proposal. If Jasmine also declared her love in an acceptance, it would create an unbreakable bond between them. I believe that makes this a strong receptor for Forrest's spirit. The garden is shrouded in rare and ancient spells. This may overcome whatever magic that Scordato has used to hold Forrest. We know that Forrest's magic is strong enough to briefly penetrate this shield of entrapment. The Garden of Mystery is our best chance for Jasmine to have a strong connection to her true love. It may be just enough to allow Tremble's detection abilities to be able to focus on where he is being held."

"You are so wise, Inezia." Tremble pulled the woman into a strong hug. "We are so fortunate to have you with us."

"How do we get to this Garden of Mystery? Will we have to pass through rough terrain?"

Tremble smiled to herself as she listened to Jake's questions. He was now military through and through.

"If we had to walk there, we would certainly have to pass through some difficult areas." With a slight smirk on her face, CeCe began to answer Jake's question. "Actually, I am not sure how we would get there from here on foot."

Jake's look of confusion caused Tremble to offer an answer.

"Jake, I do not think that there is very much foot traveling in Neverwrong. Those who are magically inclined have ways to travel that eliminate that need."

"I'm not going to say what is going through my mind as I have enough sense to know that it is not polite and is probably a creation of Hollywood. I will just ask, how do you travel?"

"He is wise beyond his species." Jasmine gave Jake an approving smile. "For long distances, we transport ourselves with magic. For short journeys, we use apparatus that is similar to a hover board. It has made an appearance in mortal movies."

"Oh, yeah. I remember that. Cool." Jake's smile caught Tremble off guard. Her heart did a little flip.

"Are you okay, Tremble?"

The momentary change in her expression did not go unnoticed by Jasmine. Her mother gave her a wink as Tremble made eye contact.

"Yes, fine." Tremble cleared her throat. "So, when shall we depart for this new location?"

"There's no time like the present." Jasmine looked around the group. "Will you be accompanying us, Inezia?"

"Yes, I believe I will. I might be able to offer some insight regarding what transpires. You might find it interesting to know that I have never been to the Garden of Mystery."

"Who created this Garden?"

"Excellent question, Tremble. It was the dream of Abelia to have such a garden. Abelia is the second oldest of the sisters. She was a great studier of the ancient spells. I believe there is a story that she read something in one of the ancient books about an intricate spell creating a beautiful garden. This garden would hold great wisdom and be the place where eternal enchantments could be created. It could also reveal the secrets of complicated mysteries."

Tremble pondered Inezia's words. She wondered if more than her father's location could be revealed by the visit.

"Tremble, I would like for you to travel with me, as we journey to the Garden. CeCe will take Jake. Inezia, are you okay to travel on your own?"

"Certainly, just blaze the trail for me to follow."

Jasmine called them all into a circle. Those who were travelling together held hands as Jasmine began a long and complicated spell. Without any warning, Tremble felt her feet leave the ground and Jasmine's grip on her hand tighten. They were propelled straight up into the sky like a rocket. After the initial burst of speed, their travel seemed to slow a little. Tremble could feel Jasmine's hand, but she could not see her.

"I am right beside you, Tremble. Just hold on. It will only be a few more seconds."

All of a sudden, Tremble felt herself being pulled away from her mother. She lost her grip on Jasmine's hand. A chilling feeling swept over her as if she was being dipped into ice. Her view changed from the white fog that she had seen all around her to a green atmosphere that felt prickly and uncomfortable.

"I am more powerful. I will kill you again. No child has the magic to overcome the GREAT—"

Just as quickly, the gravelly sounding voice was gone, the green turned back to white, and Tremble's feet hit something hard.

"What happened? Why did you let go of my hand?"

Before Tremble could get her bearings, Jasmine had hold of her by both shoulders and was shaking her. As Tremble's vision adjusted to the scene around her, she found herself looking straight into the terrified eyes of her mother.

"I don't know. You were talking, and then all of a sudden I was being pulled away from you." Tremble looked around and saw that the others were standing behind Jasmine. "Everything changed. The air got heavy and green and sharp. I was suddenly extremely cold. I heard a voice, a scratchy deep voice."

"What did the voice say?"

In a flash, Inezia was behind Tremble. Her sudden movement made Tremble jump.

"Let me think." Tremble quieted her mind as Laken had

taught her and concentrated on what she had just heard. "It said, 'I am more powerful. I will kill you again.' That makes no sense."

"Was it a male voice?" Inezia questioned her further.

"Yes, it was male and very gravelly. Almost like something was impeding him from talking."

"Did he say anything else?"

Tremble looked intently at Inezia and tried to remember.

"Right before everything changed back, he said one more thing. He was cut off though before he could finish. He said, no child has the magic to overcome the GREAT—. That was it."

"What are you thinking?" Jasmine let go of Tremble and followed Inezia as the woman began walking away from them. "You think it is him, don't you? No one summoned him. How could he possibly be here?"

"Calm down, Jasmine. We are in the Garden of Mystery. You know that rare and ancient powers were used in its creation. It is possible that Abelia created something within this atmosphere that would allow all magical powers to be able to come to this place."

"But, his powers were highjacked. He stole them."

"True, but that does not make them any less powerful. All he has done, thus far, has been to remove the power from others. It seems Tremble's account shows he was only able to connect so far with her and then something stopped him."

"It is hard to know what secrets this garden holds without doing more research into how Abelia created it."

CeCe joined them. Tremble saw that Jake appeared to be standing at attention behind her.

"Oh, Laken would know this, or he would quickly be able to find out. I wish he was here with us. Oh, how I wish it."

Tremble began to cry as the words left her. The ground be-

gan to shake and lightning flashed in the sky. The wind howled
like a wolf and darkness engulfed them. Tremble heard her own
cries change to screams. She felt two arms surround her. It was
Jake. She knew that it was Jake.

Just as quickly, everything stopped. Soft light shone down
from the blue sun. As she looked in front of her, Tremble saw
something shining. The light that was coming off it was blinding.
Everyone was shielding their eyes. She heard Jake cry out as if
in pain.

"STOP!"

Tremble's word was loud and forceful. The light ceased. She
rubbed her eyes as she could not believe what she thought she
was seeing. Tremble broke away from Jake's grasp and ran to
where the light had been. She stopped in her tracks as she got
within arm's length.

"Is it you?"

"I think so."

Standing before Tremble was her friend, her Protector. No
longer was Laken imprisoned in the Garden of Stone. No longer
was he a statue there. Tremble reached out to touch her friend.

"No, Tremble, wait."

Jasmine's words stopped Tremble. She stepped back as Jasmine, Inezia, and CeCe approached Laken. There was an elabo-
rate amount of spells. Tremble could see the magic flying through
the air. She stepped back further and found herself engulfed in
Jake's arms. His eyes were filled with concern as she looked up
at him.

"I don't know what I did. It must have been powerful."

"I've never seen anything like it, Tremble. You looked like
you had all the powers of heaven at your disposal. It was a com-
bination of every electrical storm I have ever seen paired with a

sci-fi movie."

Sparks continued to fly in every direction as primarily Jasmine and Inezia performed all sorts of spells on Laken. CeCe was mainly standing back in amazement with an obvious amount of fear flowing through her. Finally, they nodded at each other and stepped back. CeCe ran up to Laken and embraced him.

Over CeCe's shoulder, Laken's eyes met Tremble's. He was in a total state of shock. Slowly, he returned the embrace around CeCe. As she stepped back, Tremble escaped Jake's grasp and began walking toward her Protector. With gentle steps, Laken did the same. His gait was as if he had not used his legs in a while.

Tremble held out her arms and Laken slowly walked inside them. His stiff body instantly relaxed when she encircled him in the embrace.

"I never thought I would feel that again." Laken whispered in her ear. "I wished for it every minute. Then, I heard your voice, and I was free."

Tremble stepped back from Laken and looked into his eyes. He seemed caught off guard by her reaction and reached out to her. She tilted her head and continued looking into his eyes. She wasn't sure what she was searching for, yet, she knew she would know it, if she saw it.

"You heard my voice?"

"Yes, you said 'Laken would know this,' then I heard you say 'wish,' instantly I was moving. I was terrified for the first few moments until I saw your face. It was leading me."

Tremble turned and looked at Jasmine and Inezia. The looks on their faces told her what she already suspected—they had no idea what had just happened.

"Why is everyone so confused?" Laken looked around.

"Queen Perpetua foretold of the Child of Power. I know you realize that must be Tremble. Did you not study what she said the child would be able to do?"

"Laken, I have indeed studied Perpetua's writings." Inezia looked both relieved and tired. "Throughout those extensive pages, I do not recall her saying that the Child of Power would be able to bring anyone back from the state you were in."

"No, it did not say that. It did say, though, that the Child of Power would be able to do miraculous feats of magic, all from the love within the child's heart."

Laken locked eyes with Tremble. Before her peripheral vision saw him, Tremble could feel Jake's eyes watching. She could also feel the pain in his heart.

Chapter Seven

"I**T IS GLORIOUS THAT** Laken has returned to us, but we have gotten way off task here."

Tremble detected a nervousness in Jasmine's voice. Attention had been drawn to Laken since his miraculous return from the Garden of Stone. They had been in the Garden of Mystery for over an hour and had not explored the area around them.

"We have all been in such shock." CeCe joined Jasmine where she was standing. "You are right, Jasmine. There will be time later to learn about Laken's experience. We must shift our attention back to why we are here."

"There is not much to learn about my experience, Your Royal Highness. It is as you have all described. I was in a frozen state. I could see you and hear your conversations. There was no physical pain to it, other than when it first occurred. Even that was just a feeling of hardening. The pain in my heart was considerable. I cannot imagine how Claudia and Marcellus have stood it these hundreds of years. They must surely have turned mad early on. Madness would be your only escape."

Everyone was silent for a few moments. It gave Tremble the opportunity to look around at their surroundings. The garden was beautiful and lush. Layers and layers of vibrant colors were visible everywhere in the vegetation. Tremble's eyes caught a vivid green flower floating by and the color reminded her of something.

"Laken, do you still have the pendant?"

All eyes went from Tremble to Laken in lightning speed. She watched as Laken reached down and felt for the necklace that was around his neck during his stone state. It was gone.

"I don't remember feeling it leave. It must have happened during the transformation."

"Another aspect of this that makes no sense, no sense at all."

Tremble rose from where she was sitting and began to pace. She decided it must truly be a trait she inherited from Jasmine. Her mother was wearing a similar path on the ground opposite her.

"Tremble, what does the pendant look like?" Jake's silence was broken by the question.

"The pendant was created by Inezia. It is in the shape of a butterfly. She made—"

"Look around your neck."

"As I was trying to say, she made eight of them. One for each of Claudia's and Marcellus' children. I have the one that was Perpetua's. She was my long ago grandmother."

"Yes, I know that. Someone told me that. I can't remember who." Jake scratched his head. "Look around your neck."

"Again, this one is—"

Tremble's words were cut short as she reached for her pendant. Looking down at what her fingers were already feeling, she found that around her neck were two pendants. The one with the purple stones that had been given to her by Jasmine was in its open position—all the stones were visible in the full wing span of the butterfly. On top of it, lay the one that had been around Laken's neck. The wings of the butterfly were in the clasped position, but the green stones within it glowed brightly.

Tremble's hand began to shake as she touched it. Quickly, she released it. As it landed on her skin, she felt the heat coming from it. The pain of its impact made her jump.

"You need to get that thing off you."

Jake moved toward Tremble and reached out to grab it. Instantly, Laken was standing between Jake and Tremble. His arms were outstretched to block him. From over Laken's shoulder, Tremble saw the smoldering anger that was growing in Jake's eyes.

"STOP! Both of you stop!"

Inezia's command was coupled with a bolt of lightning that shot up into the sky as her arms reached in the same direction.

"Move out of my way, young men." Neither one of them moved as Inezia headed toward them. "I said MOVE!"

The old woman no longer gave them an option. With the sweep of her hand, they both flew in opposite directions away from Tremble. Inezia approached Tremble and studied the object around her neck.

"What do you think?" Jasmine spoke from behind Inezia. "Is it him?"

"I have no doubt. I cannot imagine how he was able to get it to Tremble after Laken came back."

"No, she had the pendant before that."

Everyone turned in Jake's direction. He was still sprawled out on the ground where Inezia had thrown him.

"What? Jake, what do you mean?" Jasmine walked toward Jake and magically brought him to his feet.

"When we first got here and you were trying to find out how the two of you got separated, I saw the pendant around her neck. I was going to say something about it. Then, everything happened so quickly with Laken."

"It was transferred to me before I wished for Laken's return?"

Tremble's mind rewound to when she was separated from Jasmine. She felt the icy cold prickly feeling that had passed over her body. She saw the green heavy mist all around her. Her body felt the pull of some unknown force.

"I don't remember receiving the pendant. There were too many other conflicting feelings at that point. Everything about that brief time was so strange and uncomfortable."

Jasmine and Inezia exchanged looks with CeCe. Tremble thought that all three of them looked like they were about to say something.

"Go ahead and say it." Tremble paused and again looked at them. "I will then. I had this pendant on when I wished for Laken to be here. Do you think it was the pendant that made him return?"

"Tremble, I honestly do not know." Inezia took a very deep breath. She did not look well. "I created these pendants to be a protection for those who would wear them. I did not intend for them to have any power to do anything. As you know, this green one that now adorns your neck was in my possession all of these many years until Laken took it a few days ago. Whatever has changed with its power has done so since then."

"After you left the garden, I kept thinking that I wasn't

alone." Laken stood up from where Inezia had thrown him. "I could only see straight in front of me. My hearing was limited as well. Sometimes I would think that something was passing in front of me. It would be a very quick blur in my vision. I thought it might be a bird. Maybe it was Scordato."

"None of this makes any sense."

CeCe walked over to Laken and touched him. Tremble wondered if she was still finding it hard to believe that he was there in front of her.

"Inezia, the pendant is still glowing brightly." Jasmine pointed to Tremble. "What do you think might happen if Tremble opened the pendant?"

"Maybe this retched thing would stop glowing. Every time I move I feel a little scorch on my skin."

"I just don't know. I can't imagine how it is even being made to glow. I have the globe that is attached to it—"

In a flash, their view changed and Inezia was in a room that Tremble did not recognize. She watched as the woman walked toward a bookcase. Her arms rose up above her head.

"How in the world did he find it?"

Inezia's arms came down. Tremble heard a swishing noise as if Inezia was taking a knife and cutting through the very air around them. Their view changed back to the garden.

"Let's open the pendant. It is obvious to me now that Scordato has something to say."

Jasmine walked toward Tremble. Inezia pushed her away.

"It is not for you to do. I shall do this. My fingers can stand whatever magic that is coming out of it better than yours would."

Inezia looked deep into Tremble's eyes. She instantly felt a calm feeling come over her. She took a deep breath and nodded to Inezia. The woman carefully took hold of the pendant, flinching slightly as she maneuvered the clasp. Tremble noticed that the design was slightly different from her own pendant. The wings were larger and had a bolder filigree that gave a glimpse of the stones within.

With a snap, Inezia opened it and the wings spread out to create a pendant that was almost twice the size of the one Tremble had been wearing. All the shades of green imaginable glimmered from the large and small stones that were set into the butterfly.

Instantly, a hologram-like image stood before them in the middle of the garden. At first, its green color hid the view of the image; slowly, the profile of a man became visible. Tremble immediately recognized him.

"My dear Tremble, you have grown into a beautiful young woman. I see your mother's delicate features and your father's stubborn determination in the very expression of your face."

Everyone remained still and silent. The image of Scordato turned around and looked at each of them.

"Dear Inezia, you so lovingly cared for us as children, a mother to us. It is a shame that you chose to abandon us after our parents were taken. This all might have turned out so differently if you had been there to influence those who chose to leave me forgotten."

"The influence of The Evil could hardly be overcome by just one enchanter."

"Influence!"

Scordato's voice rose. The limbs of the trees around them shook.

"Such foolish talk! Nonsense. I was influenced by no one. My power is all of my own creation."

Scordato turned again and cast his gaze on Laken.

"Ah, my son. It pained me so to see you in the state of my

parents. It was not *I* who caused you to be in such a state, but the wicked magic of the one who created the pendants. I wonder still if she is not in partnership with The Evil that took the great Marcellus and Claudia."

"I AM NOT YOUR SON!"

The power in Laken's voice almost matched that of Scordato's. Tremble felt Jake move in beside her and take hold of her hand.

"You can deny it all you want, but the truth shall not be hidden. Belladonna is such a naïve woman. She believed that everything was under her control. It wasn't, was it, Jasmine? Or should I say Your Royal Highness? The very words are like bile in my mouth."

"Where do you have my husband? Where are you hiding Forrest?"

"Ah, Forrest, the great warrior, the man of technology. His Achilles heel is no doubt his love for you, my dear. He was a hard one to find. I do so love a challenge."

"You will love tangling with me then."

Tremble could no longer keep her mouth shut. Scordato whirled around to face her.

"Oh, my darling, I look forward to it. How is your little dog? Let me think, what did you name her, Chow Chow? She was the runt of the litter, sickly. I could empathize with her fate."

"Why don't you come out from behind that holograph or whatever it is that you are hiding in and face me right here and now?"

Inside Tremble's mind she could hear several people telling her to be quiet. She shook her head.

"Oh, I am afraid that this Garden of Mystery, as dear Abelia named it, is off limits to me. I cannot imagine that my sweet sister created it to be so, yet, my powers are not able to penetrate this location."

"It's a good thing you can't because I would kick your a—"

Jake's anger could no longer be squelched. He was in front of Tremble and lunging for the hologram image.

"Jake, stop!"

Once again, Jake fell to the ground. Jasmine pushed him back with magic.

"Oh, yes, you are the mortal boyfriend, aren't you? I thought that we had gotten rid of you when Laken sent you off to join the human military. I see that you have tagged along for Tremble's big adventure. So many of your kind have come to the magical world to follow one of our beautiful people. It surely will not take long to rid our world of the likes of you."

"You had nothing to do with my influencing Jake. That was my idea and mine alone."

"Of course it was, Laken. You were so experienced in taking care of magical princesses living in mortal worlds." Scordato's tone was dripping in sarcasm. "Your devoted heart just thought that idea up. Tsk, tsk, you couldn't stand the thought of a little competition where Tremble's heart was concerned. I felt it was my fatherly duty to help you."

Laken was the next one to try to get to Scordato. This time it was CeCe who stopped it. She then asked her own question.

"If you are not able to enter the Garden of Mystery physically, how were you able to create a way to enter here this way?"

"This delightful technology was created by Forrest. He is quite the whiz with magical advancements."

"Forrest? I cannot believe that my husband willingly created anything to help you."

"I didn't say that he did it willingly. I have plenty of ways, ancient and new, to make others do what I want. Some are painful to the mind and some are physically horrendous. On certain occasions while he has been in my care, Forrest has sounded just like his grandfather, my twin Baldric. Those have not proven to be pleasant days for young Forrest. Not pleasant at all."

Tremble could see a fire engine red aura forming around her mother. CeCe's aura was black. Inezia's had the tone of actual flames; the orangey glow almost looked like she was on fire.

"You've obviously come here for a reason. Do tell us what that is." Tremble's tone was bold and direct.

"Precisely. I do like your tenacity to get to the point of a matter." Scordato's image began to walk in circles. "You have now come of age. It is time for us to get this grizzly matter of the fulfillment of the prophecy out of the way. I am ready to assume my rightful position as the Supreme Ruler of Neverwrong."

Tremble started to contradict him. A strong 'stop' came into her mind from Inezia. As she glanced at the woman, Inezia shook her head.

"I realize that you and your mother shall be seeking to find Forrest. It shall be a grand family reunion. You haven't seen your father since when?" Scordato paused for effect. "Never!"

Again, Tremble heard loud words of caution in her mind. She was beginning to get dizzy from all the brain noise. While she was momentarily distracted, Jake ran toward Scordato. Laken was the one to pull him to the ground this time. That only managed to tick Jake off.

"You stay out of this. I am here to protect Tremble and that's what I intend to do."

Laken seemed to have regained any loss of dexterity that he might have suffered during his stone time. In a move that totally contradicted what he had just done, he pushed Jake in the chest with what it appeared to Tremble to be his own strength, not magic.

Jake fell into the hologram of Scordato. He hollered out in pain as the magic image was passing through his body. Instinctively, Tremble stretched out her arm and pointed at the hologram. From her fingertips flew piercing silver beams that disintegrated the image. She rushed to Jake. He was unconscious.

"Mother, do something!"

Jasmine ran to them and knelt beside Jake. Putting one hand on his forehead and the other on his stomach, Jasmine began to softly hum. The sound grew in intensity until, at last, Jake opened his eyes.

"What happened?" His voice was groggy.

"You were knocked out by magic, my dear." Jasmine smiled down on him. "Scordato has run off."

"I wouldn't be so sure of that, Jasmine."

Everyone turned toward the sound of the voice. It sounded like it was at the edge of the woods. A weaker version of the hologram began to glow.

"Tremble's magic is strong. There is no doubt. She is no match for my power though. I will make the next part of your journey simple. I will lead you to Forrest."

"Why would you want to do that?" Tremble stood up and walked toward him.

"Because I am losing my patience. I have waited several hundred years for you to arrive. I am tired of waiting. I will be more than happy for you to meet your father. I shall make the introduction."

"That will not be necessary. I shall introduce my daughter to her father."

Jasmine rose from where she was kneeling with Jake. Instantly, her attire was changed. She had on a long, beautiful cloak. It was iridescent black and dark blue. Hundreds of tiny diamonds sparkled from within the fabric. It twinkled even in the low light of the room. The collar of it spiked up to her ears. On her head was a gold crown with large jewels of every color within its design. Underneath the cloak, Jasmine wore a skintight navy jumpsuit and black pointed boots that rose above her knee. She looked regal and rambunctious simultaneously. Despite the somber moment, Tremble couldn't help but smile.

"Oh, Jasmine, I am sure that is your heart's greatest desire. Unfortunately, I do not plan to allow that to happen. I have other plans."

Tremble glanced at her mother and saw that her eyes were now like slits and her expression was that of pure anger.

"No, I do not believe that you shall be there when Forrest's eyes first gaze upon the beauty of your daughter. I shall be there. But, you, I do not think so."

"You just said that you were going to lead us to my father."

"No, I said that I will lead *you* to Forrest. I will not make you take the journey alone though. I will allow you to bring champions along. I thought it would just be one, my dear Laken. Now, I see that you have a mortal protector as well. I shall allow you to bring these two young men with you on this journey to your father."

"I AM GOING WITH HER!" Jasmine's voice shook the ground underneath Tremble's feet.

"You may shout that as loud as you wish, it shall not change the outcome. If you do not allow Tremble to go find Forrest without you, none of you will *ever* see Forrest *alive* again. This is not an idle threat, this is a promise. He is under my confinement. As powerful as Forrest is, he is not in the position to do battle with me. If he was, he would have already done so, don't you agree?"

Tremble heard her mother take a very deep breath. It was so deep Tremble wondered how her lungs held all the air that was used.

There was silence. No one moved a muscle. Tremble could feel the twitching of magic all around her trying to be suppressed.

"Silence. Finally, you have seen that I am in charge here. It is a wise move on your part. It shall make this whole transition much easier."

Scordato paused. He began to walk in circles again. When he reached Tremble, he stopped. The light of the hologram was fading. She could clearly see right through him.

"I do not want to harm anyone. You are my family. I will be happy for you to serve under my rule. I desire for us to be one big happy family. You have had no role in what Baldric did to me. Even though you have descended from him, I hold no grudge against you or your parents or any of the extended family of these generations."

Tremble maintained her stoic expression. This time, it was Inezia whose voice she heard clearly. 'Stay calm.'

"I will leave you now. Rest. Take care of the mortal's injuries. Allow Laken to reclaim his fleshly state. I will send you a message within that pendant and it will lead you to your destiny." Scordato turned to Jasmine. "Do not test me, Jasmine. I will destroy everyone you love with a blink of my eyes. I will fulfill the prophecy myself if you choose to cross me. You have protected this dear child for many years; do not make that all for naught by one foolish action."

Scordato turned his attention back to Tremble. A smile crossed his face. He snapped his fingers and was gone.

Silence continued for several minutes. No one moved. Everyone seemed to have the same thought—the possibility that Scordato was still lurking nearby.

"Don't try to talk me into taking you. This is Scordato's game; we will play by his rules."

"For now."

Jasmine turned and walked toward the same bench that Inezia had been sitting on. As she sat down, Tremble noticed that all the leaves above her head were filled with frowns.

"That tree reads emotions, doesn't it?"

"It does, Tremble. It is a Feeling Tree." Inezia sat down next to Jasmine. "The Garden of Mystery is where the truth is told. Untruths are not welcome here. It is the reason why no matter how much it pains and angers her, Jasmine will abide by Scordato's rules. She knows that he spoke truth here; he had no choice."

"You believe everything that loser said. I would not trust him." Jake had recovered from his incident and was leaning against a tree.

"Young man, I will not argue that Scordato has nothing but ulterior motives." Inezia began what sounded to Tremble like a speech. "But, you must understand something clearly and completely. Magic is pure and powerful. The enchantress who created this garden had a very specific plan for its use. She used some of the most ancient spells known to the magic ones. She created a haven for truth and permanence. Try as Scordato might, he cannot sidestep the spells that govern this place. Even in his state of glimmer, he could not tell even a half truth."

Jake bowed his head and nodded. Tremble could tell from his body language that he was not in complete agreement with Inezia. Yet, she also knew that his manners would not allow him to contradict the older woman further.

"Well, if all of that is true, then he wants to be reunited with his relatives. That sure would be some family reunion." Tremble shook her head and chuckled.

"You have got to be wrong, Inezia."

All eyes turned to Laken's outburst. It even generated a shocked look from Jake.

"You can wish it, but it does not make it so."

"No, I CANNOT be his son. I am the son of Anton, a Protector who died with valor."

Tremble noticed that CeCe had become very quiet and was looking very pale.

"Laken, I understand that you do not want this to be your reality." Jasmine rose and walked to Laken. She put one arm around him. Her voice was soothing, calm. "It will not help for you to be agitated about it. You must soon go with Tremble. You must do the job you were created to do."

"What if I have been created to do evil instead of good? What if he tries to use me in some way?"

Tremble was afraid of what she saw happening. As she started to speak, Jasmine sent her a message to wait. Jake walked over to Laken. At first, Tremble's Protector looked slightly scared. He regained his demeanor and gave Jake a solid stern look as he got closer.

"It's no secret. I don't like your connection to Tremble. I don't like what you did to me. I don't like how you dress. I don't like you. But, I think your motives are pure. You have her best interests at heart above all else. I don't think this warlock has been pulling your strings. Man up. Remember what they trained you to do. I would just as soon take Tremble to wherever by myself. I know though that I don't have the magical prowess. That's where you come in. I am the Man of Steel. You are the Man of Magic.

For this round, we are on the same team."

Tremble felt tears rolling down her face as she watched Jake hold out his hand to shake Laken's. At first, Laken looked at the huge outstretched hand as if he did not understand what he was supposed to do. Inside her mind, Tremble said 'shake his hand.' Whether he heard her message or realized the proper action himself, Tremble was not sure. His stern look changed to a smile when his slender hand was grasped by Jake's large one. A truce had been created, at least for now.

"Excellent. I believe we should all try to rest. CeCe, get out the tablet and let's endeavor to communicate with Dana and Bridget. I'm sure that Tremble would like to speak with her mother before this next phase begins."

As Jasmine finished speaking, Tremble walked up behind her. She encircled the woman with a hug from behind resting her head on her mother's back.

"No matter what happens, I'm glad I got to know you, even if it was just for a little while."

Jasmine turned to Tremble and returned the hug. She held Tremble's head on her shoulder for several minutes, stroking her hair and softly humming.

"We have come too far to turn back now. We must finish what we started. There has always been risk. Tonight, despite his mocking arrogance, I saw a vulnerability to Scordato. I saw a glimmer of what young Amadeus must have been like. I think you have the power to overcome him. Perhaps, he might even have a second chance at his first life. It all depends on how much of The Evil is guiding him. There is one sliver of knowledge that we must keep solidly in the forefront of our minds—he does not know that he is being influenced by The Evil. This makes him all the more dangerous."

Jasmine walked to the center of where they were. She began to twirl around in a fast motion. As she did so, everything around them began to change. Tremble closed her eyes as the movement was making her dizzy. When she opened them again, within the garden was a huge room. Tremble was struck by how futuristic it looked. On the edges, the beautiful garden remained, but within this futuristic circle, there were cubicles for each of them to slumber in.

"Wow! This beats the heck out of any barracks I have been in."

Tremble watched as Jake walked toward one of the cubicles. There was a panel suspended in mid-air with a button on it. Jake looked around, smiled, and pushed the button. Instantly, the cubicle area began to open and a bed appeared. It was also hanging in mid-air.

"This looks rather small for someone my size." Jake looked at Jasmine.

"Put your hand on the center of it."

Jake did as she asked and instantly the bed was a larger size—Jake size.

"Cool." Jake hopped up in it and got comfortable.

Tremble was getting ready to explore one of her own when CeCe motioned to her.

"I'm talking to Bridget." CeCe made the screen room so that everyone could see, if they wished. "Yes, Jake made it here just fine. A lot has happened since we arrived. We are all tired, so I will be brief. Laken is okay."

"Laken? What do you mean? He was imprisoned in stone. What happened?"

Tremble could see the concerned look on Bridget's face change to curiosity and surprise.

"The short version of this is that we are now all in the Garden of Mystery."

"Oh my, that's interesting."

"Yes, and during our trip here, Tremble was pulled away from Jasmine."

"What? Tremble was what?" Dana came into view with a scared look on her face.

"I'm okay, Mom." Tremble walked up behind CeCe so that Dana and Bridget could see her. "Nothing happened to me. Well, I guess that isn't quite true. I'm not sure what happened to me exactly. I wasn't hurt though."

"Was it Scordato?" Dana's questions continued.

"Dana, we are not sure. Whoever it was also freed Laken." CeCe turned around and motioned for Laken to come into view. "Here he is. We are all just amazed and happy."

CeCe's words again made Tremble realize how everything that had happened made her emotions for her surrogate son come to the forefront. CeCe might like to give off the image of being aloof and stern, yet, there was a caring side to the woman as well.

"Why are you in a mystery garden?"

Tremble smiled at her mother's mix-up of words. It was, perhaps, as good a description as the formal name. Bridget turned to Dana to clarify.

"They are in the Garden of Mystery. It was created by the second oldest sister of The Seven. Abelia was well versed in the ancient and rare spells of the magical world. It is said that she created this garden as a place for only the truth and that anything that happened there was destined to be permanent."

"Bridget is right. We think we saw some evidence of that today. We had a visitor—Scordato."

Both Dana and Bridget gasped as they heard CeCe's comment.

"He was in hologram form, via technology designed by Forrest. So, we now have definite confirmation that he is holding him. It was an interesting conversation to say the least. Bridget, I will send you a download of my memory later." Bridget nodded as CeCe took a deep breath. "Here's the part of this conversation that you are not going to like to hear. Scordato is going to lead Tremble to Forrest."

"And? There's got to be more to that."

Tremble looked at her mother as Dana made the comment. She was wringing her hands.

"The only ones who can accompany Tremble are Laken and Jake."

"Why?" Bridget looked puzzled.

"We do not know the answer to that. I would imagine though that it is some punishment probably for Forrest. As the descendant of Baldric, he is the one who Scordato is probably most interested in hurting. He even made the comment that Forrest reminded him of Baldric."

Tremble noticed that CeCe was leaving out that Scordato had said that the days that Forrest sounded like Baldric turned out to be hard days for Forrest. She was glad that CeCe was censoring the information for her mother.

"I have nothing against either Laken's or Jake's abilities to help Tremble, but, it would seem to me that Jasmine or yourself are much more trained to do battle with the likes of Scordato."

"I'm sure that has played into Scordato's reasoning. Unfortunately, there is not much that we can do. He has vowed to destroy everyone that Jasmine loves if she defies him."

"And you believe him?" Dana made a scoffing sound. "He

could be bluffing. Why should he tell you the truth?"

"He had no choice but to tell the truth in the Garden of Mystery, Dana." Bridget answered the question before anyone else could. "Abelia created it to be a place where truth could not hide. He means what he says."

TREMBLE'S DREAMS WERE fitful. Scordato was holding Choo Choo off the edge of a cliff. VeVette had wings and was flying around the room. Andrew was operating on Elvis. She woke up with the feeling that she had not slept at all. She just about jumped out of the bed as she realized that she was not alone.

"You must have had some crazy dreams."

Jake whispered from where he was sitting on the end of her bed. Tremble realized that her bed was now larger than it was when she went to sleep.

"What are you doing here? You should be sleeping."

"I've gone for days without sleep in the Navy." Jake paused and began absentmindedly playing with Tremble's feet. "I wanted to tell you something while we had the chance to be alone."

"Okay." Tremble swallowed hard and bit her lip preparing for whatever he was going to say.

"I know that Laken has the advantage where we are going. He's the one who knows the magic."

"Jake, don't worry about—"

"Let me finish. I just want you to know that I thoroughly understand that I might not come out of this alive." Tremble shook her head. "Trem, it's a real possibility. None of us might, but me most of all. I won't be able to defend myself the same way you all will. I want you to know that it's okay and I understand. I don't want to be anywhere else."

Jake moved closer to Tremble and held her face in his hands. The sparks that she felt rising all over her, this time, had nothing to do with magic.

"I love you, Tremble Dawson, to the moon and back." He laughed and put his forehead against hers. "To Neverwrong and back."

"I love you, too, Jake."

"That's all I needed to hear. Don't worry about me, if something happens. Don't blame yourself. It's like going off into the war zone. There's risk. I intend to fight long and hard. But, someone wins and someone loses. I won't be the loser in this case though, as I will have had you."

Jake leaned in for a long kiss. The moment made her feel carefree and young. She realized that she had just turned twenty-one, yet, she felt so much older. Tremble wondered if she made it through this journey alive, if she would ever feel young again. She heard it said that experiences could age you faster than years. Judging on that theory, it scared her to think how old she would be on the other side of Neverwrong.

"You look like you are a thousand miles away. I was hoping that kiss might keep you focused on me."

Tremble smiled and leaned in for another kiss. There was something very different about Jake. The kiss was different from the one they had shared on the night of her birthday. It was as if there was an electrical current going through him. She stopped mid-kiss as a thought caught her off guard.

"What's wrong?" The look on Jake's face changed from contentment to concern.

"I just thought of something that I need to ask Jasmine. I will have to try to remember to ask her before we leave."

Tremble swung her feet over the edge of the bed and touched the door of the cubicle. Instantly, it opened. Peering out, she saw a gray mist all around them.

"I wonder what time it is."

"Couldn't tell you." Jake looked down at his wrist. "My indestructible Navy watch is destructed." Jake smirked. "Guess it didn't survive too well through that intergalactic journey I took. I wonder where we really are versus Earth."

"They tell me that this is just a parallel universe. They say we are still on Earth."

"And you believe them?" Jake shook his head and jumped off the bed.

"Well, either this is a very long dream or it is real. I've got to be honest, I kind of wish it was a dream."

"I really wish it was a dream. You and I would not be here. I am thinking we would be together on some college campus." Jake reached out to lift Tremble off the bed. "Wait, this is summer, we might be on some great vacation."

"Or working some boring summer job."

"Couldn't you stand a little boring right now?"

Jake's words hit home. Boring did sound very appealing.

"Knowing what I now know, it is hard to imagine a different life, though. It is incredible to think that I have two sets of parents. It is mind-blowing to realize that I have this whole other history in another world."

"It is terrifying to think what this other life will do to the one you had."

Tremble understood. Jake was afraid that her magical life would take over her mortal one. His fears were justified. It already had.

Tremble was at a crossroads. If she survived what lay before her, she would look back on it as the day that changed everything. She was going to step into the battle that was her destiny.

Tremble put her arms around Jake and laid her head on his chest. Their height difference had always been a matter of joking. He was a good foot taller than her. She felt his strong arms encircle her. In the familiar position that should have been a feeling of comfort, her mind began to wander. Then it started to race as a thought came to her with great clarity.

"Before we go where Scordato wants us to, there is somewhere else I need to go."

As she let go of the embrace, Tremble stood back and looked into Jake's eyes. She saw love mixed with confusion.

"I've got to go to the Library. You are going with me. You and Laken must both go."

She did not wait for him to respond. Walking out of the cubicle, Tremble looked around to those of the others. A couple of the doors were open. She could hear movement as she saw the sun rising between a cluster of trees.

"You are up early, my dear."

Tremble turned around to see Inezia working her magic on a breakfast scene for them. A large table came into view filled with delicious looking foods.

"I don't smell coffee."

"We don't have coffee here."

"Well, can't we get some?"

Tremble heard Jake chuckle behind her. He was well aware of her love affair with the dark drink made of beans.

"I'm afraid that you cannot make something appear that does not exist here." CeCe joined them. "I have petitioned for it. None of our Royals have seen fit to become coffee drinkers."

"Oh, well, that stops now. Do I have the power to make this

happen?"

"No, my dear daughter, you do not. I am still the Supreme Ruler of Neverwrong."

No matter how many times she had now seen Jasmine, Tremble was still awe-struck by her beauty. Flawless skin, beautiful hair, impeccable style—Jasmine would be a tough act to follow.

"Coffee is very natural. It's a bean." Tremble gave her a big toothy grin.

"It also is caffeinated and we do not caffeinate in this world."

"I would ask for decaf, but who am I kidding?" Another chuckle came from Jake. "What's so funny? You should own stock in Starbucks."

"Hey, I love coffee, no doubt. It's just funny seeing you without it. Your magic isn't working, Princess."

Tremble stuck her tongue out at him. Behind him, she could see Laken approaching. He looked rather rough.

"How come he can call you Princess? You chewed my head off for doing it."

"Well, the difference is that he has always called me that, even before he knew I was one."

"I always knew, babe. You were always a princess to me."

"Oh, please. This is making me sick." Laken rolled his eyes. "I'm starving."

"You look like you didn't sleep a bit."

"Oh, I slept. My dreams, however, kept me up. It was like I was reliving my time in stone."

"Hey, man, you should probably get some counseling for that." Jake joined the conversation as he began to fill a plate with food. "PTSD is some serious stuff."

"What?" Laken's plate was growing in content as well. He stopped to give Jake a puzzled look.

"Post Traumatic Stress Disorder. It is a very serious condition. We learn all about it in the military. You have something as stressful as what happened to you, you need to get some help."

"We need to overcome Scordato and get life in Neverwrong back to normal."

"I'm not sure what that means, Laken, but, I do want to overcome Scordato and The Evil that is influencing him. Before we are led to Forrest, I think it might be a good idea for me to visit the Library again."

"What makes you think that?" Jasmine sat down at the table. Tremble joined her.

"I'm not sure." Tremble paused and thought about it. "I really don't know why I feel this way. It's an instinct, I suppose."

"Or perhaps it is the influence of one of your ancestors."

Inezia was seated on the other side of Jasmine. CeCe and the two young men sat on the far side.

"I believe that there is something in Perpetua's letters about how she might guide the Child of Power at a turning point in the kingdom's history. This certainly qualifies as a turning point."

"Inezia, I remember that." Laken stopped eating and got a look on his face that Tremble likened to sorting through files in his head. "I believe she said something along the line of that she would come out of the darkness to lead the Child of Power to the light."

"That settles it. After we finish eating, the three of us are going to the Library." Tremble smiled as she began to fill her own plate.

"Three who?" Jake mumbled as he chewed.

"Three, as in you, me, and Laken."

"Why him?" Jake and Laken said simultaneously.

The action caused Jasmine, CeCe, and Inezia to all laugh.

Tremble took a deep breath as she realized even this simple action was going to be a problem.

"I believe my question is more appropriate." Jasmine gave the young men a raised eyebrow look before she turned to Tremble. "Why don't all of us go?"

"Well, I suppose that would be fine. I just thought that Jake and Laken should stay nearby me in case the pendant starts vibrating."

"Jake may not even be allowed into the Library." Laken's voice was overly smug.

"And, why would that be?" The aim of Jake's glare was precise.

"You are a mortal. The Library is a magical place. You probably would not be allowed access."

Tremble did not like the tension that was brewing between the two people who were going to be her sidekicks for the most important part of her journey. Her mother read her thoughts and relayed back to let her handle it.

"Laken is right." Another smug look crossed the young man's face. "But, as the Supreme Ruler, I can allow access to anyone of my choosing, magical or mortal." Laken began to look deflated. "I agree that the two of you should stay with Tremble wherever she goes from here on out. We will all go to the Library."

Jasmine put some magic behind her words. Before Tremble could take another bite of her breakfast, they were all instantly within the walls of the Library.

"How did we—"

Jake's comment was accentuated by the shocked look on his face and the way he appeared to be pushing the air down around him. Tremble laughed.

"Don't laugh at me. You still have a fork in your hand."

Tremble had not realized that her right hand still contained the fork she was using. A piece of fruit was still on it. She popped it in her mouth, and then made the fork disappear.

"Excellent!" Laken gave her a thumbs up. "You are now making things disappear with ease."

"Can you make people disappear?"

"That's it. You two young men come stand before me." Inezia had obviously had enough of the testosterone banter between Jake and Laken. "Come on. Don't make me bring you here."

The two walked to the center of the room and stood before her. Both assumed a military stance. Tremble had forgotten that Laken also had such a background. She caught them eyeing each other's posture.

"The two of you are here for one reason and one reason only. Do you know what that reason is?" Laken's mouth opened to answer. Jake began to mumble. "Silence! If I wanted you to speak, I would ask you a question."

Tremble tried to stifle a giggle and heard CeCe doing the same behind her. Jasmine gave both of them a look of warning.

"You two are here to take care of Tremble and help her in any way possible. Petty schoolboy jealousy and adolescent behavior are not acceptable."

Each of them started to speak. A quick wave of her hand stopped that from happening. They tried to speak again and no sound would come out of their mouths.

"Your focus will be on Tremble's well-being. You two shall cease all of this warring between yourselves. You only war with Scordato and The Evil. Understood?"

Laken and Jake sheepishly nodded at Inezia and bowed their heads.

"I will be watching from afar. Tremble, do you wish me to keep them on silent mode?"

Tremble laughed out loud at the woman's comment until she realized that Inezia was serious.

"No, I suppose it might be helpful for them to be able to talk to me."

"Very well, your wish is my command. I think you would enjoy it more this way." Inezia turned out of the boys' sight and winked at Tremble. With a wave of her hand, she lifted the spell.

"Yes, ma'am." Jake's voice came out in a stutter. "I will keep on task and not cause Tremble any aggravation."

"Tremble's well-being is my utmost goal. It is why I was created. I was made for Tremble."

"Watch it, Laken. Even though a factual statement, that was borderline. I suggest that both of you practice silence."

Tremble walked around the room, shaking her head.

"Now, let's get to the reason why we came here. I think that there is something in this room that will help me. I just don't know what it is. During one of my early views of this room, I was shown Scordato taking command of the volumes here. I am wondering if my power shall allow me to do the same thing."

Tremble looked at Jasmine. Her mother smiled and nodded.

"I think that it is worth a try." CeCe sat down in one of the armchairs. "Perhaps something will be revealed to you."

"That's what I thought. Here goes nothing."

Looking around the room, Tremble saw that most of them had stepped back and were either leaning against a wall or sitting in a chair.

"Jake, you might want to not stand in front of a bookshelf."

Jake quickly moved out of the way as Tremble closed her eyes and began to concentrate. After a few moments, she raised her arms and opened her eyes. The books seemed to come to life. Sparks of light and energy flickered from them in an array of colors beyond description. It was beautiful and frightening at the same time. With her arms still held up, she glanced at her mother. Jasmine seemed to be in strong concentration as if she was trying to help Tremble. Jasmine gave her a brief smile and Tremble heard a whisper in her mind. She repeated the words.

"Legions of knowledge, I command you to speak to me."

One by one, all of the books flew off of their shelves and began spinning. The beams of light and brilliant colors continued. Each book seemed to search its own pages for information. Gradually, each one of them stopped twirling and went dim—all of them, but one. It flew to Tremble and hovered in front of her. Its light changed from golden to purple to green. It opened in front of her to a particular page and grew still.

Tremble lowered her arms, reached out, and the book placed itself in her hands. As she peered down at the pages, she saw that the light had highlighted a certain area.

"Read it to us, my dear." Her mother's voice was barely above a whisper.

"And his name shall be Scordato, the forgotten one. He shall overcome those who have forsaken him. A child shall be his deliverance from captivity."

"That is the core of the prophecy." Laken interrupted her. Inezia shot him a look.

"Read it again, my child, you will not be interrupted."

"And his name shall be Scordato, the forgotten one. He shall overcome those who have forsaken him. A child shall be his deliverance from captivity. A child of power shall free him from the bonds of evil and be a light of renewal. He shall not perish if his heart is pure. The child shall be the heir to all things. The heir shall reverse an act of love. The mightiness shall cease."

Tremble stopped reading. The book flew out of her hand, closed itself, and vanished.

"Oh my, where did it go?"

"It could be back on one of these shelves or it may have destroyed itself." Inezia rose and walked around the room look-ing at the shelves that were once again filled with hundreds of books. "I imagine the latter as it has waited all of these years to be read by you and you alone."

"May I speak?" Laken's voice was firm.

"Yes, Laken, tell us what you think. You have studied this passage as have I." Jasmine nodded to him.

"I have read this passage, but not all that Tremble revealed. It ended after the first few sentences."

"Indeed, from my reading, also."

"May we go over this together? Perhaps, it shall help us to review what we already know. And, to review for those who do not know." Laken nodded curtly to Jake.

"I think that is a good idea, Laken. There is much to under-stand."

Tremble stepped back and sat down on one of the sitting areas built within the bookshelves. Looking around at her angle, she wondered if she was sitting on the very enclosure where young Amadeus was left to die. A cold chill passed over her, causing her to twitch. She looked down at her pendants. They were still.

"And his name shall be Scordato, the forgotten one."

This time, instead of a screen, Laken created an easel-type object to view the passage as they went over it.

"We, of course, know that Scordato was once Amadeus. He is the oldest of the children of the Supreme Enchanter Marcellus and Her Royal Highness Claudia, and the twin brother of Baldric. Amadeus was thought dead and left in this very room when his siblings went down the mountain and formed the kingdom we know as Neverwrong. Amadeus experienced some of The Evil that entombed his parents. He lived within these walls for many years and consumed the knowledge on these shelves as it pertains to all of the magical world. This is where he became Scordato and planned his revenge. That brings us to the next sentence."

Laken paused and another portion appeared before them. Tremble noticed that Jake seemed very deep in thought.

"He shall overcome those who have forsaken him."

"This is where it begins to become real for all of those who have descended from The Seven."

Inezia interjected her thoughts. Tremble noticed that the woman exchanged a look with Jasmine. She also saw Laken bow his head and wondered if he was thinking about his questionable heritage.

"Hold on a minute. Before we go any further, I am not sure that I know how this prophecy was relayed." Tremble stood up and walked toward Laken. "It seems that this book I just had includes much more than just the few sentences that you knew prior to my arrival. Have you actually been able to view this book before?"

"No, we have not. Each Queen from the generation after Perpetua has tried and failed to find such a book." Jasmine had a faraway look in her eye. Tremble wondered if her powers were taking her to each of those previous queens.

"So who communicated this message to you?"

"It was Meserve."

"I have heard that name before. Who was he?"

"Meserve was a close companion of Marcellus and Claudia. He came with us when we journeyed from our homeland." Inezia rose to answer. A screen came into view next to her with the image of a man on it. "Meserve had unmatched power. After Marcellus and Claudia did not return here, one by one we sent out some of the servants to look for them. The servants never returned. Finally, Meserve went out on his own. He returned to get me as he had seen what had become of them."

Inezia sat down again. It appeared that the act of recounting that time was too much for her. Her somber expression brought out the age in her face. Hundreds of years was a long time to carry such dreadful memories.

"I do not know this for a certainty, but it is what I have come to believe. Meserve took me to the Garden of Stone. Amadeus and Baldric followed us. For some reason, Meserve walked into the woods. He was not with us when Amadeus reached out to his mother. Afterward, Baldric brought Amadeus back here, and I stayed with Marcellus and Claudia. I am not sure what happened to Meserve. It was not until some years later, through my powers, I saw that Meserve was again here in this room with Scordato. I was able to view their interaction. He seemed to hold Meserve responsible for his fate as well as his siblings."

"Where is Meserve now?" Tremble leaned on the arm of the couch where Jasmine was sitting.

"We do not know. He has not been seen for a very long time. We fear that Scordato has limited his contact with the Kingdom of Neverwrong." Jasmine took hold of Tremble's hand. "He may have imprisoned him as he has done so with your father."

"He could probably shed a great deal of light on everything. If he has been under Scordato's control, then he would certainly know things about him no one else would." Tremble paused and became lost in that thought. Everyone was silent. "Oh, how I wish I could meet and talk to Meserve."

A crack of thunder jolted everyone out of their thoughts. They all looked up at the ceiling. Tremble watched as a multicolored galaxy appeared above their heads. Flashes of light were followed by what Tremble would describe as meteors. The changing view, for some reason, reminded Tremble of the passage of time. The actions ceased as quickly as they started. The ceiling reverted back to the way it was and quiet returned.

As Tremble looked back down, she noticed that a large and very old looking chair had appeared in the center of the room. The back of it faced all of them. It was made of wood with gold inlaid in the carvings. An eagle with its wings spread was carved into the back.

Slowly, Tremble rose to approach the chair. Out of the corner of her eye, she saw Jake begin to move in that direction. With her left hand, she motioned for him to stay back. A message came to her as she reached the back of the chair. It was Inezia. 'Do not be afraid.'

Taking a deep breath, she continued to walk around to the front of the chair. All Tremble could see was the bowed hooded head of a small person with a dark brown robe on. She could not see the person's hands as the arms were folded in front of the chest and the hands were within the opposing sleeves. The robe went down to the floor and pooled around the legs and feet. Standing there for a few moments, she did not see any movement. Jasmine slowly came around to the edge of the side opposite to Tremble. 'Say his name.' She gave her mother a confused look as she received the message. 'Meserve.' Tremble's eyes grew big.

"Meserve."

Still there was not any movement. Tremble bit the bottom of her lip and thought for a moment. Taking the pendant in her hand that had been passed to her from Perpetua, Tremble knelt in front of him and repeated his name again.

"Meserve."

The pendant vibrated for a moment. Slowly, the head before her rose. At a snail's pace, two hands came out of the robe and moved to grasp the arms of the chair. The hands were small with long bony fingers. The skin was translucent. Tremble thought she could see the man's blood pulsing through his veins. One by one the long fingers tapped the end of the chair arm.

Tremble sat down on the floor and scooted back a little. She could tell from her view that this person could probably see her through the folds of the hood. Yet, her view of his face was still concealed. A quick glance behind him revealed that all of the others looked as if they were ready to pounce in her direction, if needed, but were held in a state of suspension until then.

"Claudia." The voice was raspy and low. "You are the image of Claudia."

Tremble squinted her eyes and tilted her head as she looked up at Inezia. The woman had drawn closer when she heard the voice.

"I have noticed. You favor our dear Claudia when she was in her maiden years."

The head turned slightly as Inezia spoke.

"That is a voice I know. It is older, ah, it would be. Doomed to a life as long as I. Punished for being alive."

Tremble heard a faint chuckle, followed by a cough. It sounded as if a rattling was coming from his lungs.

"Mr. Meserve, sir, may we see your face?"

Tremble's fear was being overcome by her impatience. She

scooted back to him and peered closer. His right arm slowly reached for the hood. It looked like the movement was quite an effort. Jasmine drew closer to him.

"May I?" Her voice was soft and soothing. Jasmine was in her healing mode.

He lowered his arm again. Tremble thought she heard a sigh of relief.

"Yes. Thank you."

Jasmine reached behind the man and gently pulled the hood down. His head was bald and wrinkled. His skin looked like dust. It was as translucent as his hand. You could almost see his bones, like a skeleton. As he raised his head, he opened his eyes. Tremble gasped. They were bright and beautiful and the most unusual color of green.

"Green. Your eyes are very green." Tremble's thoughts came out of her mouth. She made eye contact with Laken. He gave her a look of understanding.

"My eyes reflect the life I have led. It has been long and troubled, full of expectation, with no conclusion." Meserve turned his head slightly as he looked at her. The bones in his neck cracked like the sound of a tree limb breaking. "Who are you, my child? You must be one who has come from the beauty of my dear Claudia." Before Tremble could answer him, his eyes saw Jasmine. "Oh, you are the vision of Perpetua. It is more than my heart can bear."

Tremble got concerned about his last comment and motioned for Inezia to come closer.

"Relax. He is cursed for a long life. A little shock to his heart will not take him."

"Ah, Inezia, your wit was always sharp and your aim was precise. I have missed you, my old friend."

"I would like to know where you have been all of these years. Tremble is the one who has summoned you, so you must do her bidding first."

"Tremble? That is a strange name for this beautiful child?"

"Yes, sir. I will agree with you wholeheartedly about that." Tremble drew closer to him so that she could have his full attention. "Why is it that I was able to summon you from wherever you were?"

"I would imagine that you might be the Child of Power that our dear Perpetua wrote about. If you are indeed that child, then you have the power to summon anyone who is a subject of this part of the magical world."

Meserve reached for Tremble's hand. As he grasped it, she was surprised at how warm he was and that his grip was quite strong.

"I have been waiting to meet you. I have been waiting a very long time." Meserve squeezed her hand. "So, my beautiful child, what is it that you seek from Old Meserve?"

The old man smiled. There were no teeth to shine in his mouth, but his smile was no less beautiful to Tremble. He had a warmth to him like she had never experienced.

"We were studying the prophecy that you wrote long ago. It seems to be my destiny."

"Yes, my dear. It is a blueprint to how you shall change the destiny of all those who have come before you and those who shall join us afterward."

"It would be lovely if you could tell me what I should do." Tremble gave him a big smile.

"I suppose that it would seem that way. Unfortunately, I cannot do that. The order of things must play out as it should and can only move forward with your wisdom, instinct, and free will."

"Oh, he's good." A silent Jake offered his perception.

"He is the wisest man to have ever graced Neverwrong history." Laken added, nodding in agreement.

"Despite my advanced years, I will have you know, young grasshoppers, I am still in the room. My body has long since left its most useful state, yet, my mind has the agility of youth. Please talk to me, not about me."

"Meserve, I wished for you to be here so you could help us understand this prophecy in some way. Can you do that?"

"Yes, my child, I will try."

"We have already discussed and I believe we understand the first few sentences. I will read the entire passage to you."

Tremble nodded to Laken and he made the entire passage appear on the easel.

"And his name shall be Scordato, the forgotten one. He shall overcome those who have forsaken him. A child shall be his deliverance from captivity. A child of power shall free him from the bonds of evil and be a light of renewal. He shall not perish if his heart is pure. The child shall be the heir to all things. The heir shall reverse an act of love. The mightiness shall cease."

"It is a riddle, is it not?" Tremble saw a subtle smile cross Meserve's face as he spoke.

"Yes, and I do not care much for being part of a riddle, especially one that has me and Scordato being the two main characters."

"You only see two characters there."

"Yes, it begins with Scordato, and then talks of a child."

"Only one child?"

"What?"

"My dear, a prophecy is not a simple thing. It is not the obvious you must understand, but that which lies beneath it."

"Oh, my stars in heaven!" Laken shouted and started looking closer at the easel. "This is about Scordato and at least two other people, isn't it?"

"What are you talking about?" Tremble took her head in her hands as if it hurt.

"Wouldn't that be something?" Jasmine stood next to Laken as she reread the passage.

"What do you know about me?" Laken kneeled down in front of Meserve.

No sooner had the question come out of Laken's mouth than the green pendant started vibrating around Tremble's neck.

"Uh oh." Tremble pulled it away from her chest by the chain.

"Please answer me, sir. I beg of you."

"I know that you are not who you think you are. You can be who you want to be."

"More riddles." Tremble stood up. The green in the pendant was getting hotter and vibrating quickly. "Can't anyone in this world give a straight answer?"

"You do not want a straight answer, Tremble. You want an easy one." Meserve's words were sharp. "I will give you one that has bitter truth to it. It may be hard for you to swallow."

Tremble had begun to move away from Meserve. She was still holding the pendant away from her body. She stopped in her tracks.

"I'm listening."

"This is not a riddle. This is not a prophecy. I have seen the future. This is a truth you will have to live with forever after it occurs." Meserve paused and breathed deeply. Tremble heard the rattle again. "Because of you, someone will live. Because of you, someone will die."

As Meserve's words registered with Tremble, she momentarily forgot about the pendant. It slipped from her fingers and hit her chest hard. She heard a sizzle as she let out a scream.

Chapter Eight

"THAT IS SO SOOTHING, Mother."

Jasmine was immediately at Tremble's side when she screamed. The green pendant had left a butterfly wing-shaped burn in the center of Tremble's chest. The pain was excruciating until Jasmine put her healing hands upon her daughter.

As Jasmine lifted her hands, Tremble thought about Meserve's final words to her.

"Oh, that's strange." Jasmine's voice was laced with surprise and concern. "Come look at this, Inezia."

Tremble looked down at her chest as the old woman joined them.

"No way." The burn was completely healed. Yet, the impression of the butterfly wing remained, like branding. "This is not good. Make it go away. I do not want Scordato's brand on me."

"He has entwined a deep spell into this pendant." Inezia ran her finger over the impression. The action gave Tremble a feeling similar to an electric shock. "I cannot imagine how he was able to bypass my magic to do this."

Tremble watched and listened as her mother recited numerous spells. Inezia joined Jasmine in the effort. Nothing seemed to be working. The pendant continued to glow.

"I think we better go ahead and open the pendant." Tremble looked at Jasmine. Her mother stepped back and nodded. "Are you ready? We may have to leave quickly once we get these instructions. I really wish I could have prepared more."

Laken and Jake nodded. Tremble thought that both looked a little green.

Carefully, she released the clasp that held the wings of the pendant in place. At once, the green light was shining on all of them as the jewels that were contained within it became visible and sprang to life. For the briefest of moments, Tremble forgot what was happening as she saw that everyone around her now had a green face.

Tremble looked back at the pendant. It was twitching and glowing, but nothing else was happening. She waited a few moments, still nothing.

"I thought that Scordato would have been quick and exact with his message."

"He shall not do as you expect him."

Tremble had almost forgotten about Meserve until the old man spoke.

"What do you mean?"

"He is in control now, true control. Once you go and find your father, the games begin. You might take that control away from him."

"Hold on a minute, old fellow. How is it that you know Tremble is supposed to go with Scordato?" Jake walked back over to where Meserve was still sitting.

"I know everything, young man."

"How can that be?"

"My life has been a curse in more ways than just my lifespan. I have been cursed to see all. It would have been a special thing to see happiness befall the family of my dearest Marcellus and Claudia. Yet, happiness has not been something of generous supply with any of the generations, then or since. I have seen all that has crossed their paths. Even the dissension which has occurred within their own blood."

"Sir, if you know everything, then what's going to happen next?"

Tremble could not imagine that Meserve would answer Jake's question.

"The prophecy is more than a riddle, more than a mystery. It tells a story that must have a beginning and an end. Yet, the writing of it is not finished any more than the actions themselves. The Child of Power will write the end to this saga. But, that child will not be the only one who is holding the pen."

"Another riddle, Meserve, another riddle." Jasmine began to pace. "I am tired of them. Tired, I say! My whole life has been consumed by them."

This was the first time that Tremble had seen aggravation from her mother. Like her, sparks shot out of her finger tips in a variety of colors. It made Tremble smile inside to see this connection she had with her mother.

"You want another life? You are not alone. It is all the good that would go with all the bad though. So wish carefully."

Meserve began to slowly rise from his chair. The sound of his bones creaking reminded Tremble of the popping and cracking of firecrackers. She wondered how old he was. It was not the time to distract him with such a question. Once he was upright, he began to speak.

"You must go and face what shall be. Knowing Scordato as I do, I must advise you that you may find this interaction frustratingly slow. Even though he has waited his whole life for what he imagines to be his victory, he will want to savor this time."

As Meserve finished speaking, Tremble heard the chime of a clock. It was a strange sound to hear. She had not remembered seeing a clock anywhere in Neverwrong.

"The time has come, Tremble." Scordato's voice sounded as if it was being projected through a loud speaker.

Before Tremble could move, Jasmine was by her side embracing her. A message came loudly into her mind. 'Do not let your guard down, even for a moment. Try to communicate with Forrest with your mind. It will be the only way to do so undetected. I love you more than life.' Jasmine quickly backed away before Tremble could respond or even embrace her mother further.

Almost as quickly, Laken and Jake were on each side of her. They each took hold of her hand. The pendant began to vibrate at such a speed that the flashes of green light became blinding. The brighter the light became, the firmer each of their grips became. Before her, she could barely see Jasmine, Inezia, and CeCe. With a quick glance, Tremble saw that Meserve was walking toward them. Suddenly, he disappeared. Tremble closed her eyes and opened them again, thinking perhaps they were playing tricks on her. But, the old man was no longer there. Tremble heard the snap of a finger and neither were they.

As Tremble, Laken, and Jake were being transported to the unknown location of Forrest, the mode of travel felt as if they were rising. It was a weightless feeling coupled with a strange consciousness.

In the dreamlike state that she found herself, she heard Dana. It was a memory from her childhood. Her mother was in a PTA show. It was a fundraiser for new playground equipment at Tremble's primary school. The parents had put on the musical *Grease* to a packed high school auditorium. Her normally reserved mother was cast in the role of Rizzo. It was a night of awe for Tremble as she saw a side of her mother that she never knew existed. Tremble wondered if this little blip of memory was sent to her by her mother for the purpose of making her smile. The image of Dana in tight leather pants and teased hair belting out a show tune was a welcomed commercial during a stressful moment.

As her mind awakened more, she felt the firm grips of Jake and Laken on each of her hands. She wondered if she dared to speak their names.

"Jake? Laken? Can you hear me?"

"I can hear you, Tremble. I doubt that Jake can."

Laken's answer frightened her.

"Why? Is something happening to him?"

"If you can still feel his hand, I think he should be okay. His mortal auditory system is probably not allowing him to hear very much. I would imagine that he is in a semi-conscious state."

"That's the way I sort of felt for a while. I think I'm still holding on to both of you though."

"Your brain knows that you need to hold on, so it keeps telling your hands that. I would liken it to when you are asleep. Your brain keeps you from falling out of bed."

"What is happening to us? This all seems to be taking a long time."

"This experience reminds me of my military training. Scordato is probably taking us through this as a distraction."

"I don't understand what you mean."

"This upward movement that you feel is what it is like to go into another dimension. I experienced this during my military training because our magical opponents might try to send us somewhere else as a form of imprisonment. That may be what Scordato did with Forrest. Yet, it wouldn't explain how Forrest was able to communicate with you via your dream. It takes powerful magic to communicate across dimensions. That's what makes me wonder if this is a ruse."

"Aren't you concerned that he will hear this conversation between us?"

"Why? After you first said my name, we have been communicating via our minds ever since."

The realization shocked Tremble. Making her wonder if her magical abilities were advancing as everyone had told her they would.

"Your power is increasing by the minute, Tremble. I can feel the change."

Up until that point, Tremble would have described the view as nonexistent. The motion was so fast that everything they might have seen was just a blur. Tremble could feel it changing. They were slowing down.

"Get an extra good grip on Jake." Tremble could feel Laken moving toward her. "I'm going to see if I can maneuver to take hold of his other hand. The impact of reaching another dimension can sometimes throw you into orbit if you are not prepared for it."

"What is this doing to his body?"

"Nothing. Our bodies are basically the same. We can withstand this travel. He doesn't know what to do from a magical sense. That sense is within him though, so we can help him."

Laken drew closer to Tremble. Moments later, the three of them were in a tight circle. Their speed slowed further as Tremble saw glimpses of color and shape. Her feet hit something hard and they bounced to a stop.

"Oh, this cannot be happening." Laken's tone was disgust mixed with humor.

Tremble's eyes began to adjust. She first looked at Jake. His eyes were as big as saucers and his complexion was a little green. Otherwise, he looked okay. She squeezed his hand and he looked at her. A smile crossed his face.

"Why are you holding my hand?" Jake turned and saw who was on his other side.

"I was trying to keep you from flying off into another world." Laken made a great show of releasing Jake's hand. "Look around you; it appears as if that long trip was for nothing."

Tremble let go of both of their hands and stepped away from them. The surroundings were very familiar. Hauntingly familiar. They were back in the Garden of Stone.

"What? This was all a wild goose chase?" Tremble extended her arms out and turned around in a circle. Her hands clinched into fists. "Scordato! SCORDATO! You have some explaining to do."

It started off softly. The sound rose as moments passed. It was laughter, heckling laughter. The laughter of a madman. It was a sound heard in every horror movie Tremble had ever watched.

"Oh, the Child of Power is angry, is she? Things not going

as you would like? Everything that I have allowed you to see has been an illusion. Everything you have wanted to see has always been there."

Shooting a look at Laken, she realized that he was now standing where he had been imprisoned in stone. He had returned to that form. Beside him was Jake, frozen in statue form.

"NO! NO! NO!"

Tremble's screams came from the depth of her soul. She crumbled to the ground and pounded on it with her fists.

"I suppose that I could extend to you my sympathies and apologize for my behavior."

Realizing that the voice had changed, Tremble stopped screaming for a moment and listened closely. She did not raise her head. Her senses became attuned with everything around her.

"I will not waste my time on deception. We have much to do."

The voice Tremble was hearing was female. It was the voice of Belladonna. Slowly, she raised her head. There was no one in sight. Tremble's mind raced, searching for what she should do.

"Aunt Belladonna, is that you?"

"Ah, playing the family card now, are you?" The voice seemed to be coming from the trees above Tremble. "I am Belladonna and I am not. Can one person be two?"

From deep inside her mind, her memory began sorting through all that it knew. It felt like someone looking at thousands of files at once. Some of the memories were obviously not her own. Had someone bestowed others on her for this purpose? Tremble saw a vision flash before her eyes. It was a young Belladonna kneeling beside a body. She was crying. A beautiful man approached her and offered comfort. The man turned and

Tremble could see his face. She had seen him before.

"Sebastian."

The laughter resumed. It was menacing. It was lyrical. It was female. It was male.

"The Child of Power is a wise one. I thought it might be the musings of that old man and the first queen of my kingdom."

"Your kingdom? I think not. It does not belong to you because you try to take it."

Tremble rose from the ground. As she did, she felt an incredible surge of power pulsate through her body. Instinctively, she knew from where it came. It was Claudia, Perpetua, and all the firstborn females. It was Marcellus, Baldric, and all the firstborn males.

"It shall be mine. I have commanded it."

"Where is Scordato? Where is the forgotten one? Have you forgotten him also?"

A ray of green light appeared before her. It was a hologram of Scordato.

"Is this who you are calling for?"

The hologram materialized to the form of Scordato that Tremble had seen in the Library with his siblings. He was adorned as a king in fine clothing and jewels. The image changed to a frail man in rags who had first revealed himself in that same scene. A few moments passed, as Tremble continued watching, the figure became a small boy laying in a small enclosure. His breathing was shallow, almost undetectable. Sebastian appeared in the room.

"Oh."

It was the only word that escaped Tremble's lips for the understanding of what she had seen.

"It's more than a parlor trick, my dear. How did someone who had no magic of his own perform such an illusion that it fooled an entire world? You tell me. It is all in my name, my real name. I foretold it all with one word. When you discover my name, we shall begin."

"Where are you? Do you have possession of Belladonna? Do you have my father imprisoned? All this time, I thought I was fighting Scordato."

"You were fighting an illusion."

"But, you do exist. They know you are The Evil that destroyed the beginnings of their family. They know you are the reason that Marcellus and Claudia originally fled their homeland."

"Yes, their homeland. What was the name of that place?"

"No one dares to say the name."

"For fear that I will be summoned." No longer did the voice even have the hint of a female tone. It was now deep and dark. It howled with laughter. "I have always been here. I have been just beyond their sight. Waiting. Waiting."

"Waiting for what?"

"For you, my dear—the Child of Power."

"I don't understand. Did you not create that part of the illusion? Did you not create the prophecy that foretold my existence?"

"Another illusion. This one I did not create. This one is on the head of Meserve."

All the while that Sebastian had been talking, Tremble had moved around the garden. Her movements were automatic. Her depths of listening had been seeking out the location of the voice. Tremble realized that she was standing between the stone figures of Marcellus and Claudia.

"So who is Meserve then? I have been told he was a close companion."

"A companion, he likes to portray that. Everything changed when they fled from the homeland. They changed everything." Sebastian paused. "The color of the sky, the color of the grass— Marcellus thought that if he changed everything, it would make the reason they fled go away. He thought he could create a mirage of what was and everything would be better. Meserve and Inezia knew that would not be the case. Meserve prophesied the truth of what would come to be."

"Inezia. She was your wife?"

"I had to create a way to seal my security in the world of magic. Aligning myself with Inezia and Meserve did that quite nicely."

"Inezia and Meserve? There's a connection between them?"

"Oh, my dear, they have hidden so much from you. It is a shame. It has hindered you so. This long life that they both have lived has nothing to do with me. It is not a curse. It is who they are. Meserve and Inezia are father and daughter. Meserve is the source of all the power that was in their magical world."

Tremble sat down between the two statues. Her mind was exhausted and her body surrendered.

"Inezia took you to her homeland. She showed you how it once was, correct?"

"Yes."

Tremble repositioned herself between the two statues as she did so her hands briefly touched each of them. She felt a surge of power pass through her, and then a feeling of warmth. She dared not show this on her face.

"Meserve was the ruler of that land. It's supreme power. I could not believe my great fortune to stumble into this world and to become the object of love of the daughter of such a being. I knew then that it was *my* destiny to be the supreme ruler of all the magical world."

"Even though you yourself possessed no magical ability?"

A crash of lightning lit up the sky. A roll of thunder followed it.

"It was robbed from my people. Our magic was taken from us. I am the one to take it back."

"I do not understand how you can take it back. You syphoned the power from all of the people in Inezia's homeland. I saw the empty shells of them with my own eyes. Why not just kill them? Surely, there is some miniscule part of you that understands the horror of it all. You have suspended them in the misery of an entrapped life."

"It is the only way that the power will continue. No magic will flow through them if they are dead."

"No magic will flow to *you*, if they are dead. That is what you really mean. You are a leech that is living off of the lifeblood of others."

"It will all change soon."

"How will it change?"

Tremble gazed up at the face of Claudia. A drop of water fell from her face. Tremble wondered if it was the morning dew or a tear from the woman's heart.

"Your death shall give me my life of power."

The words slapped Tremble in the face. She felt the ground move under her. She had placed her hands on the ground to brace herself to stand. The earth underneath had split and cracked. It was her own power that caused the rumble. It was a sign.

"Where is my father? Where is Forrest, the King of Never-wrong?"

Her racing mind told her that she must distract Sebastian from the topic of her death. She must keep searching for what would free her from the situation.

'I am here.' A deep voice spoke in her mind. It was the same voice that came out of her father's mouth in the dream. 'I am with you.'

"Oh, that name, it is so ironic. Did his parents know that it would be his final destination? I have wondered that."

As he answered her, Sebastian's voice moved from place to place through the trees like a bird darting.

"It was not easy to capture your father. He is very powerful. Forrest also has a temper that gets the best of him. It allowed me the window of opportunity that I needed to lead him to this beautiful garden where his beloved Jasmine had sequestered herself with my dear bride. It only took a second while his back was turned, while he was gazing on your mother's beauty through a grove of trees that allowed me to deliver the spell that would entrap him."

"Entrap him where?"

"Everywhere, my dear. Your father is all around you. He is the Forrest—these trees." Sebastian's laughter grew in intensity. "My wit is my hidden talent. A little humor in our magic makes it even more delightful."

The howl of laughter moved through all of the trees around her. As Tremble followed the sound with her eyes, she briefly saw the face of her father flash from place to place. Her eyes darted to catch up with the movement of the image. Tears rolled down her face as she understood what Sebastian meant.

"The spell was an ancient one. It is in those books that your family cherishes so much. The spell told how you could take great power and splinter it. How the being could remain and the power would flow, but it would allow whoever controlled the power to move it where he chose. This is my most ambitious work yet and Forrest is the star."

Tremble heard a growling in her mind. It was a guttural sound like an animal in prolonged pain—the pain of her father. Tremble rose and left the space between her grandparents. She only let her eyes momentarily rest on Laken and Jake. She could not allow herself to become emotionally distracted. She had to keep on her game in order to play his.

"So, why have you brought me here, then? You've made me watch you destroy my friends. Is this a slow torture on your part?" Tremble hoped this might get a rise out of him. She was challenging in her tone.

"They are not destroyed. Neither is your father. Why even our dear Marcellus and Claudia are still very much alive. I feel them every day as I use their power. I wanted you to have all of this knowledge as you make your final attempt to conquer me. I do so love these attempts by your family." There was silence for a few moments. "You see, my dear, I really hold no ill will toward you. I feel sorry for you, in fact. You are but a pawn in this game. Scordato was called a pawn, too. Young Amadeus was deemed a pawn. He was my first vessel of power. I was so young in my talents then. I'm afraid that I have seriously tarnished the young lad's reputation. Baldric's too, but he did deserve a little torture. He did leave the dying Amadeus behind. Notice, I did not say dead, only dying. Tsk, tsk, tsk. Such a pity."

'Calm. Be calm.' Tremble stopped and listened to the voice in her head.

"I'm going to send you off to see if you can gather some more useless information in the quest of this Royal Family to rid themselves of me."

"I have questions. May I ask questions? You seem to have all the answers." Tremble knew she probably should be careful. A leopard cannot change its spots. He would have to live with her sarcastic tone.

"I do hope these are real questions and not a pitiful attempt to delay the inevitable." He paused, waiting for Tremble to respond. "Very well. Ask your questions."

"If Meserve and Inezia are so powerful, why aren't they the ones you have entombed?"

"That is an excellent question. You are a smart girl, deductive in your reasoning. Bravo!" Sebastian chuckled. The sound had a strange echo. "I am truly amazed that Inezia has told you so little about the true root of all magical power. Meserve is the core of it all. History says that there were cornerstone enchanters who hold the base of the power. He was one of the originals. There's really no telling how old that fool is. Eons are probably an accurate point of reference. Supposedly, there are several others. I remember, as a child, hearing about the cornerstone of power for my world. My world, that is, before it was robbed of its power."

"It would seem to me, then, that he would be the one you would want to conquer instead of me."

"Meserve cannot die. He can never die. He is the source of the power that you have and that I intend to permanently gain."

"How can that be? I did not descend from him."

"Ridiculous! It is ridiculous what you have not been told. Do these imbeciles think that by not telling you it makes it not so? Meserve is Marcellus' father, Inezia's father. You are a direct descendant of him."

Even though her mouth was open, nothing came out. Tremble was too stunned. The layers of twists and turns in the story that was her legacy was worse than she expected. Her mind felt like it was on a rollercoaster hurling toward a fall.

"Interesting, isn't it? No one taught Laken that part."

"Does anyone even know that part?"

"Oh, those delightful folks in the portraits do. Most of them, at least."

"I've got to admit. I am very confused. You have assumed the identity of Scordato, right?"

"Sort of. I have used him for my own means. Just like I have with your dear Aunt Belladonna. She was a very willing accomplice though when I offered her the deal."

"What deal?"

"The resurrecting of her own true love."

"Xavier."

"Yes, you know that story."

"How can you resurrect him?"

"Oh, I would not be the one who does it. You would, perhaps. At my bidding, if I so choose. Before your demise."

"The heir shall reverse an act of love."

"I must say, you have indeed been a quick study. I am impressed with your mental recall. It's outstanding considering your mortal upbringing."

"Yes, a mere mortal like you. Oh, but wait, I'm not a mortal. I just pretended to be one."

Tremble heard a disgruntled grunt. She longed to see the look on his face.

"Yes, you might reverse the act of love that led to Xavier's untimely passing. Belladonna would then live happily ever after."

"You said 'might.' Why do you even care how she lives?"

"Oh, my dear, she shall be one of my loyal subjects. I shall give her some ruling power. She has been very brave and steadfast. Who knows what crazy thing your mother might have done with you if it hadn't been for Belladonna's influence?"

"How did you get her to be so cooperative with you?"

"Well, there is that undying devotion she has for her dead love. However, it was her destiny."

"Destiny?"

"Belladonna is a deadly poison. You really should know that, Tremble. It is covered in Enchanter 101. You might say that evil is in her blood."

"So, Belladonna is an accomplice because she wants her love back. Amadeus is your accomplice, too? He got out of that box in the Library alive?"

"Yes, he did. I just happened along as the siblings were getting ready to leave him. I actually had planned to do away with all of them. I watched as Baldric solemnly stood over his twin. He was devastated. Then, sweet Perpetua placed her hand on her brother before departing. All it took was that fleeting moment. Perpetua's healing powers are unmatchable. She was still young though and did not understand how to use them. No guidance from her talented mother Claudia. Amadeus' life was hanging in the balance. Her touch turned it all around. Healing takes time though. They left soon after."

"Amadeus came back to life. His family was already gone."

"Yes, he had no knowledge of me. Well, that's not true. Marcellus and Claudia had warned their children extensively regarding The Evil that made them flee their homeland. Amadeus didn't know that The Evil was me. He, of course, knew me from when we were all family. I was Uncle Sebastian for a short time. He was too young to even remember my face."

Even though she couldn't see him, Tremble knew that he was smiling. She pictured him grinning like Dr. Seuss' Grinch. She chuckled to herself as she thought of the irony of the green. Taking a deep breath, she decided to throw another question at him.

"Why didn't he just go after them?"

"I must say that I am enjoying our dialogue. Young Amadeus did not follow his siblings because I swayed him against it. I told him that they had known he was still alive and they had left him intentionally. They had forgotten him. I told him that Baldric was intent on being in charge. I knew there was some sort of rivalry between him and his brother already. Baldric had the fierce disposition of his father. I had seen that with just a glimpse into their lives when they were babies. I knew there was a fire of dissention between them that just needed stoking. Amadeus' personality was much more like Claudia before all this happened. I molded him into Scordato."

"How do I know who I have dealt with in the past?"

"You and your family always dealt with me. As I'm sure Inezia has told you, Scordato is a pawn. He thinks I am his ally. He does not understand that I am the one pulling the strings. Without my influence, he would be nothing."

"Always, it is you?"

"No, not always. The Scordato you saw in hologram form in the Garden of Mystery was the real him. An influenced version always, but he held his own in that dialogue."

There was silence for a few moments. Tremble tried to quickly gather her thoughts. She knew that he would probably not allow many more questions, if any. She hoped that he could not read her mind as she heard his next statement.

"Earlier, you alluded to something that I did not answer. I am surprised that you did not ask it again."

Tremble's eyes darted back and forth. She also began pacing as she tried to remember. The action made her think of Jasmine. She wished that—

"You asked why I spared Inezia. Let me assure you that it

was not an act of love on my part. I never loved Inezia. She was another pawn in my game. I have spared her useless life because of the devotion that her father has for her. Since I have rendered Marcellus in his present state, Inezia's well-being is the only thing that I can hold over him."

"What do you fear that Meserve will do? Kill you?"

"That is a possibility, or worse still, kill himself."

"How is that worse?"

"If he is gone, all of the power is gone. There is no more magic without him."

"He must live forever."

"Or pass it on to someone."

"How can he do that?"

"I have no idea."

Tremble felt a cold wind sweep through the garden. It made her think that another unseen being had arrived. She soon found out who it was.

"Tremble, my dear. I apologize profusely for making you wait."

The finery of his clothes and sparkle of the jewels told Tremble who was walking toward her before she saw his face. She took a very deep breath and exhaled as she tried to imagine what would now transpire between her and Scordato. As he walked toward the statues, Scordato briefly stopped in front of his mother and stared into her eyes.

"We will fix this, my lovely. It will all be better soon."

He resumed walking and was past Laken and Jake before he stopped and did a double take on their location.

"What happened here? Why are my dear Laken and that mortal one in this state? What did you do?"

Before Tremble knew it, Scordato was standing in front of

her. He was so close that she could feel the breath coming from his flared nostrils. His anger seemed to be growing and his aura was changing colors rapidly. As she looked closer, Tremble saw that the flashes of color were coming from beneath his skin, just like they had on Laken.

"I did not do anything."

"You must have done something. You still have my pendant around your neck. They did not get this way on their—" Scordato stopped mid-sentence and began looking around. He waved his hand in what Tremble assumed was a spell. "Reveal yourself."

Tremble looked all around them. Nothing happened. She thought it was too risky to tell him what she now knew. The Evil already had enough plans for her. He might make Laken and Jake crumble into dust out of sheer spite.

"I knew the time would come when it would happen. The Evil that took my parents has returned. Once I am the Supreme Ruler of Neverwrong, I shall be able to harness all of the power of the generations and combat this force once and for all. My mentor has—" Scordato stopped himself from speaking further. "I am allowing my anger to get the best of me. I am sorry that we will not be able to engage in a proper battle. I must begin fixing this immediately. I must free Laken from this state as well as my parents. Now is the time for the Child of Power to—"

'Wish yourself away, daughter. Jasmine gave you this ability for a reason.' Forrest's voice grew stronger. 'Wish yourself away. Do not go to the Library. He will easily find you there. Go somewhere in Neverwrong where you will be safe.'

'I have to wish out loud. He will know.'

'Be creative. Use the words, but imagine a different meaning. It will work. You have the power.'

'Will I ever see you?'

'I do not know, my darling. If not, perhaps, I can meet you again in your dreams. Now, hurry.'

Tremble backed away from Scordato as he lifted both hands above his head to begin what she could only imagine was a powerful and final spell. In her mind, she quickly thought about where she could go. An idea sprang to her mind and she searched for the words to take her there. She glanced over at Laken and Jake and gave them a firm smile.

"I want to see my family."

Chapter Nine

A WHIRL OF WIND blew around her creating a funnel that took her high into the air. Before she could think about the journey, Tremble was at her destination. She landed with a thump in the middle of the room. As she opened her eyes and gazed around the circular walls, lights came on. The illumination was bright and soothing at the same time. The walls were painted a deep blue. There were seven sets of drapes. Each was a rich and inviting shade. The colors created a feeling of comfort and relaxation. The light became brighter and, one by one, the drapes opened. She had been successful. She was with her family. Tremble was in the Hall of Portraits.

Seven sets of eyes stared down at her. She had landed on the floor. Tremble saw a beautiful high back chair was waiting for her. The fabric was a plush and regal purple. On the back of the chair was a design of a butterfly, the same one that hung around her neck.

Instinctively, Tremble reached for her pendant and unclasped the butterfly. The jewels lit up and began to glow. Those on the chair did the same.

"It's her."

Tremble heard the whisper of a lyrical voice. It came from the wall behind. She did not know who had spoken.

"She is beautiful."

Another voice came from the opposite wall.

"The image of our mother, Claudia."

"Indeed."

"All those long years in which Jasmine was separated from this dear child."

"And Forrest, he has not yet held his daughter."

It was obvious who spoke the last words. The deep male voice spoke of his grandson from another time—the last first-born male in the line of Baldric.

"Sit down, my child."

The light grew brighter over one of the portraits as Tremble sat down in the chair. Directly in front of her was a portrait she had seen before.

"Hello, Queen Perpetua."

"Oh, my darling girl, I believe I told you to call me Grand-mama."

"I'm sorry, I forget. Everything is a jumble in my mind."

"We know who you have encountered." Another portrait's illumination grew. It was the one next to Perpetua. "Many a day I have wished to be able to get out of this wretched frame. My desire has been the strongest today than in all the centuries previous."

Baldric's voice was rich like her father's. He sounded strong, even though he was in a physically restrained state.

"It's all so confusing. There is so much deception on so many levels. I don't know who or what to believe." Tremble leaned forward and put her head in her hands.

"We understand your confusion."

Tremble recognized the voice that came from the right of Perpetua. It was Abelia. She was the sister who created the Garden of Mystery.

"Was it Sebastian who put you into these eternal frames or your brother?"

A chuckle from behind her caused Tremble to turn and look. The woman who laughed was gorgeous. Her features were very petite. The youth that still adorned her face noted that she had physically died at a young age. She must be Gwenora.

"Does it matter? Our sentence is the same no matter who read the verdict."

"Tremble, we believe that it was indeed Amadeus who bestowed this curse." Perpetua answered the question. "We do not believe that he acted entirely on his own in the creation of it."

"Why wasn't I told about Sebastian? I should have been prepared."

"By now you know about Belladonna. We tried on numerous occasions to connect to those who were guarding you. We also tried to get to Laken. It was to no avail." Baldric paused and turned in the direction of Perpetua's painting. "Belladonna even managed to put a sensoring spell on Pet's communications to Jasmine."

"Jasmine knows about Sebastian." Tremble searched her memory for confirmation.

"Jasmine knows that Sebastian exists. She knows that he is The Evil who our family fled from. She does not know, as you did not, that he was truly the full force behind Scordato. That he is in many cases acting as Scordato or Belladonna, or possibly others in the carrying out of their actions." Baldric's voice boomed with anger.

"Sebastian's power comes from others, and he needs others for it to manifest itself as well." Perpetua's tone matched her brother's.

"He says that he is going to kill me." Tremble heard several gasps around her from some of the sisters that had not yet spoken. "He said, 'Your death shall give me my life of power.' I suppose that since I am the Child of Power, it makes my magic the ideal kind for a monster such as him to feed off of."

"Oh my, I hadn't thought of that. Had you, Pet?" Baldric's tone lightened.

"No, he only sees potential power. The obvious cannot be seen by someone who only has evil intent." Perpetua shook her head as she answered.

"What is going on here?" Tremble looked around at all of the portraits. They were nodding in agreement.

"Tremble, you are not the Child of Power that I wrote about in my letters. You are not the only heir."

Perpetua's words hit Tremble with a wave of realization. Her mind raced back to the end of her conversation with Meserve. They had talked about the prophecy. She had thought it was only referring to her and Scordato.

"Meserve said that a prophecy is not a simple thing. It is not just the obvious you must understand, but that which lies beneath it. There's more than one heir?"

"Meserve is the originator of the prophecy. I merely quoted portions in my letters. Snippets, you might say, to help future generations find the truth."

"Tremble, you are not the only heir who has come from two

lines of this family." As Baldric spoke, Tremble heard a level of disgust in his voice. "Laken has descended from the line of Perpetua and Amadeus. Belladonna is Laken's mother and Scordato is his father."

"We had suspected that Scordato was Laken's father. But, I had not considered the possibility of Belladonna being his mother. This knowledge will kill Laken. That is, if he isn't already dead."

"Tremble, my dear, he is no more dead than our beloved parents are." Abelia's soothing voice gave Tremble hope. "As much as this knowledge has pained each of us every day of our lives, it is the truth. Like the family and friends they left in their homeland, our parents are suspended in a conscious state that presently has no physical manifestation except in stone. As horrendous as that is, it is reversible. It will take a collective power never felt before to overcome it and make all of those we love whole again."

"How do you know this?" Tremble's chair turned in the direction of Abelia, so that she could speak to her directly. "What makes you so certain?"

"Meserve has told us."

"How can he know?"

"Oh, it is another horrid detail." Abelia shook her head. "It is partially the reason behind my desire for the Garden of Mystery. There needed to be a place where truth rose to the top. There needed to be a place where deception could not hide." Abelia bowed her head and was quiet for a moment.

"Be strong, sister. You can tell her. She needs to know." Tremble was not sure which of the others had spoken.

"Meserve knows because he is the one who taught Sebastian about the spell that creates this state of suspension."

"What? Why would anyone do such a thing? I thought that Meserve was good and wise. Is there anything but evil in this story?"

"Meserve is good and wise, Tremble." Baldric's voice was stern. "He was also the leader of a magic world. He had to have rules and means to control those who would try to deviate from them. This state of suspension was a punishment. It was not intended to be a permanent or even an extended state. It did serve as a way that Meserve could take control of a situation without taking away someone's powers."

"Magical timeout." Tremble snorted at her own remark.

"I am not sure what you mean by that. If you are referring to a form of punishment, then that is correct." Perpetua began to answer further. "A magical person is hard to control. Even the most powerful enchanter, as Meserve is, cannot know what spell might be coming in his direction from someone who has already committed a wrongdoing."

"Please come over here, Tremble." Her chair turned and moved in the direction of Gwenora. "I have been here the longest. I was the first one of us to physically die. Meserve appeared to me on several occasions during those early years. He came to bring comfort and hope. He explained to me how Sebastian had taken his simple spell of confinement and turned it into a prison sentence far worse than what Amadeus had bestowed on us. It was during this time that he also began to hint that our brother was not completely responsible for his actions toward us. It was little comfort to me in those early years. I was so young and could not understand why I had died and how I could possibly survive living in a painting."

"It is wonderful to be here with all of you. When I wished to be here, I thought that I might be able to learn something from you that would help me face The Evil and free all of our family who are trapped. Can you at least tell me what this name is that Inezia refused to tell me?"

Tremble's chair returned itself to the original position in front of Perpetua. She could hear the sisters whispering to themselves in hushed tones.

"The name is a summons. He would instantly be in our presence."

"I have been told that already. Yet, that name obviously has power. Perhaps, that would be useful to me."

"Our girl has a point, Pet."

Baldric stood up in his portrait setting and began pacing within it. Tremble wondered if all the Royals paced. As she watched him, Tremble tried to figure out how old he had been when he physically died. His hair was still dark and his agility seemed to be intact.

"Baldric. I am not sure what to call you."

Baldric stopped pacing and turned to look at Tremble. A smile crossed his face. "My other grandchildren called me Grandfather. That is probably too formal now. You may decide what name you wish to use. I will gladly answer to it."

Despite the reputation for having a hard personality, Tremble saw that Baldric had a gentle side. Time within that frame had surely mellowed his disposition.

"How about Grand? Simple. Regal."

"I like that. I like that very much."

"Okay then, Grand. How do you suggest that I go about learning this name without you telling me?"

"Resourceful. I like that. Your Aunt Elsavetta is the historian of the family. Perhaps, she can offer some suggestions."

Again, Tremble's chair moved with speed. This time it went

to the portrait that was the farthest away from Perpetua. Moving in so many directions reminded Tremble of bumper cars at a carnival.

The woman before her was extremely thin and pale. Tremble surmised that she must have had a long and painful illness before her physical demise. A permanent look of death hung over her. Despite this, Elsavetta greeted Tremble with a smile.

"I must say, young lady, your resemblance to our dear mother is chilling."

Elsavetta's voice was soft and scratchy. It reminded Tremble of the old women at the nursing home where she and VeVe had volunteered one summer.

"It is so strange to be told that I look like someone. I never heard that as I grew up."

"Precisely because you did not look anything like those dear mortals. Your looks were hiding in another location." Elsavetta cleared her throat. "Baldric wishes for me to relate some information to you, historically speaking, which will help you learn this ancient name of our ancestral home. There is a book within the Library. It is hidden by a spell. It is cloaked in great magic. Meserve is the one who brought it with him. It is the only book he brought. All the others came at the bidding of Marcellus and Inezia."

"Is there something in this book that could help me?"

"Oh yes, my dear. The book is full of wisdom. The core of it tells the story of how the name of the homeland was taken by the being that wished to destroy it. It is a beautiful name now associated with great evil. I will teach you the spell to retrieve it. My caution to you is a great one. Do not read the name of our ancestral home aloud. Do not even read it in your thoughts. Learn it in silence. Hide it away. When the time comes, you will only need to say it once for its power to be seen."

"I understand what you are trying to tell me. What I don't understand is how the name of their home became the name of the one who wished to destroy them?"

"As I am sure you have been told by Inezia, Sebastian came to her world quite suddenly. No one knows exactly where he came from or if he was banished from his own land. He did not have magical powers. Yet, powers he had nonetheless. It has been studied by our smartest sons and daughters. No one can figure out though what kind of powers they were."

"Are you talking in riddles like Meserve does? My mind cannot take it."

Tremble rose from her chair and began walking around the room. After a few minutes of wandering, she turned around and realized that the portraits were following her. It was a strange sight and it caused her to laugh. The action seemed to cause each of them to revert back to their original wall position.

"You are a little mobile, I see."

"Our boundaries are pronounced and do not provide us with much enjoyment." Baldric's tone was stern.

"Our brother's words are true." Abelia spoke up. "The endless story of our children's lives that we must view is more heart wrenching than enjoyable." Tremble tilted her head to one side and looked at Abelia questioningly. "When we were banished to these portraits, our brother also worked a spell for us to see the lives of those who descended from us. At first, it was interesting and enjoyable. However, we soon saw more than we wanted and could do nothing."

Tremble looked down at the pendants hanging around her neck. An idea suddenly came to her.

"There were eight pendants that Inezia made for you. I have

the one that originally belonged to Perpetua and the one that was made for Amadeus. I presume that Baldric's is with my father. Where are the others?"

"The firstborn of this generation has each of them."

"They were created to be a protection for all of you by Inezia. She knew what you needed to be protected from. I must wonder if their collective power might be enough to protect me."

"Your wisdom is great, my child." Perpetua's smile was broad and filled with pride. "Go and collect more wisdom from the book that holds the answers. We shall summon the pendants back to us. They will all be here when you return."

"All, but those around Tremble's neck, and the one that now protects Forrest."

Tremble nodded at Baldric. She scurried back to the corner where her chair had remained and listened closely as Elsavetta taught her the spell she needed.

BEING IN THE Library alone was a little unnerving for Tremble. After committing the spell to memory that Elsavetta painstakingly taught her, Tremble wished herself to her present location. The trip had been uneventful. It seemed to her that no time had passed. Her transportation skills were improving. She was coming into her magic.

"I suppose that I am on my own now. I cannot wish for anyone else to join me. It would be too risky."

Tremble knew that speaking out loud was a risk; it was a calming mechanism for her. She wrapped herself in a spell of concealment. This had been whispered to her by Verina, the baby sister of the siblings, as Tremble prepared to depart. She remembered that Verina had been the time traveler of the group. Tremble wondered if her message had a double meaning somehow.

The room was larger than she remembered. All the walls had bookshelves made of rich dark wood. Sitting areas were located in comfortable corners with not-so-comfortable chairs that were more for sitting up straight and tall than they were for relaxing. Tremble's eyes fell on the infamous shelf seat that hid the enclosure where Amadeus was left. Her feet took her to the location before her mind could think better of it.

Taking a deep breath, she started to reach for the seat in order to lift it up and look inside.

"Perhaps, I should use magic to do that."

Tremble thought of the appropriate spell. With a flick of her wrist and the whisper of a few words, the lid rose allowing her to take a glimpse of what had once been a young boy's tomb.

She leaned over the area and looked deep within the space. At first glance, it appeared empty. As she looked closer though, she saw that a sheet of paper lay quietly alone at the bottom.

"Do I dare pick it up?"

Tremble's heart was racing with the excitement of the knowledge it might contain. Her mind, on the other hand, sent out strong warnings that it could be a trap. Again, she settled on magic as her compromise.

"Rise paper rise. Show me what it is you hide."

She did not know how she knew the spell. It could be, she imagined, there were a certain number of simple ones programmed into her genetic makeup.

The paper rose as it was commanded and hovered in front of Tremble's eyes. In the script of handwriting was a short message.

Yes, I was left here.
Left here to die.
No one to hold my hand.
No one to cry.

Never shall you see the boy
Who you left then
The Forgotten One has gone away
But, he will return again.

Will you rejoice
And welcome him to you?
Or will you judge him
For the things he did not do?

That shall be your choice
Your burden to bear.
Some day you will have the chance
To prove that you did care.

The paper was perfectly still in front of her. Around the edges was the glow of magic; it made the parchment look younger than it probably was. Tremble still dared not to touch it. There could be a spell contained with it that would begin by the spark of a touch.

"I shall take you with me when I depart. I command you to follow me back to those for whom you were originally written."

Obediently, the paper followed her as Tremble walked back to the center of the room. She knew the action must be quite comical looking.

"I have procrastinated long enough. It is time for me to get what I came for. Time is wasting."

Gazing at the shelves and shelves of books, Tremble wondered about all she could learn if time afforded her the opportunity. There could be other ways to rid the magical world of The Evil that haunted it. Her focus had to remain clear on what she knew might help.

"Let's see if Elsavetta's spell can summon the book with the mystery name."

Closing her eyes to concentrate, she replayed in her mind the spell that she had learned. The words were simple and exacting, yet, seemed to Tremble to offer the possibility of other revelations.

"Land of our fathers, shrouded in mystery, hidden in time, cloaked in our history. Present yourself for me to see, I need your knowledge, I need to be free."

Tremble opened her eyes. A glow was coming from every book on every shelf intensifying the vibrant colors. Her eyes darted from one side of the room to another as the colors flickered. She began to feel slightly dizzy and an old wooden cane appeared in her hand. Power pulsated from it as it steadied her stance. She instantly knew not to fear the object.

All of sudden, the books stopped glowing. The room became perfectly still. A few moments passed with nothing happening. Tremble raised the cane in the air.

"Come, I say. Show yourself to me!"

The open lid of the shelf seat where Amadeus had been placed closed with a loud thump.

"Well, of course. It's hidden in there. Just the place I don't want to go."

Tremble walked over to the same location she had just been in. The paper followed behind her. Using the top of the cane, she tapped on the lid.

"Open up."

Nothing happened.

"Reveal yourself."

Everything was still.

"I cannot catch a break. Maybe I need to speak Elsavetta's spell again."

This time, Tremble kept her eyes open. She needed to see what might happen.

"Land of our fathers, shrouded in mystery, hidden in time, cloaked in our history. Present yourself for me to see, I need your knowledge, I need to be free."

The lid of the box flew open and a multicolored ray of light shot straight up. Tremble waited for something to happen. The light continued without the appearance of a book.

"Book, please!"

Tremble's frustration was rising. The temper of Baldric was boiling in her veins.

"I have had enough. I WANT THE BOOK NOW!"

The ray of light dimmed and a book shot up from below. Tremble reached for it. She immediately recoiled her own hand as she saw that there was another hand holding the book. She heard a menacing laugh coming from above her. Briefly turning her attention away from the book, she looked up at the ceiling. The laughter stopped. When she looked back, the lid was down and the book was lying on the seat cushion. No hand was in sight.

"Someone enjoys playing games. You better be careful. I have a few tricks of my own."

No longer fearful, Tremble picked up the book and sat down on the seat it had been laying on. Her patience was gone. She was ready to read as quickly as possible and figure out what she needed to know.

An hour later, Tremble was still reading the book. She felt herself dozing off a couple of times and had to make a glass of water appear to help stay awake. The book was full of information about dozens of ancient spells and medicinal remedies. She reached the end and closed it without finding even one name of a place.

"Don't tell me this is the wrong book. Someone please help me."

No sooner had she spoken the words than her purple pendant began to glow and vibrate. Tremble reached down and opened the butterfly's wings revealing the beautiful jewels. Simultaneously, an upside down butterfly appeared on the back of the book in her hand. As she turned it around, the pages opened. By viewing the book upside down, she saw a whole different story on its pages.

Opening the book to the first page, Tremble began to read aloud.

"Once upon a time." She shut the book. "You have got to be kidding me."

The butterfly fluttered and glowed on the cover. Her pendant vibrated as well.

"Okay, I will try again."

Tremble opened the book again. She tried to skip the first few pages. When she did so, the pages she came to were blank.

"I guess I have to start at the beginning."

Seemingly in answer, the pages flipped themselves back to the first one.

Tremble paused and thought about the warning that had been given her to not even think of the name when she came upon it.

"I shall read out loud, very carefully and deliberately. Perhaps, this shall help me recognize when I need to stop."

Tremble took a deep breath and began.

"Once upon a time, in a magical world known only to the most gifted enchanters and enchantresses, there was a man who would rise up and lead them all. His name was Meserve. It was a peculiar name indeed. Yet, it served him well and gave him distinction as any good name should do.

"The enchanter possessed great wisdom coupled with a kindness that distinguished him as one of the fairest rulers to ever reign in the magical world. He was one of the bases of the foundation of power for the entire magical dimension. He was a constant—an anchor.

"The people of this world for generations previous had stayed true to their immortal destiny and lived extremely long lives in the abundance of comfort.

"While every generation or two, a new leader was chosen, it was really a kingdom of equality. Wealth was evenly distributed and all the people of the land worked to make life easier for one another.

"The land was known for great wisdom and extraordinary magical power. Yet, it was a place of grand illusions where, at times, it was hard to distinguish the reality of the time from a created fantasy. Because of all of these attributes, the kingdom was called—"

Tremble closed her mouth quickly. The name was on the tip of her tongue. She knew that she could not let it escape. She did not even think it. Instead, she flooded her mind with dozens of other words in rapid succession. Tremble would store the word in the depth of her memory.

As she looked down at what she had been reading, she realized that the page was now blank. Flipping backward and forward through the volume only saw more of the same. Tremble closed the book. The butterfly had disappeared. Flipping it back to its original state, she was able to see the words of the book she had previously read. She flipped the book back to the odd position and now she only could see the original pages upside down. The illusion was complete. It had served its purpose.

Setting the book on the cushion as she rose and walked away, Tremble looked around the Library. The paper was still following her. It hit her in the back of the head when she stopped suddenly to look at a portrait that hung on the wall. The portrait was of Claudia. Tremble did not remember seeing the painting in the room previously. It was located on a wall in the corner without a light to illuminate it.

Claudia's face had a youthful look. Although their lives had been worlds apart, Tremble could see the resemblance that had been mentioned to her. She wished to be as beautiful as Claudia. What Tremble found most intriguing about her was the tenacity that she saw in the woman's eyes. Claudia must have been a force to deal with, magical or not.

Returning to the center of the room, Tremble knew that she should return to the Hall of Portraits. There was a nagging doubt in her mind. She felt like there was something else in the room that she needed to see. Looking over to another corner that she had not ventured to Tremble saw the row of chairs that she remembered were created by Scordato during the visit of his siblings. Walking toward them, she saw that each of them was inscribed with a name. There were now eight chairs including one with the name 'Amadeus.'

The last chair in the row was also the smallest. It was Verina's. Thinking about the enchantress, who had a short time ago whispered a spell of concealment in her ear, Tremble sat down in the chair. Before she could take in the view of the room from that angle, the chair began to shake.

The shaking continued until it reached the intensity of what Tremble imagined an earthquake felt like. She clutched the arms of the chair. The movement was so fast that she could not take in what was happening to her surroundings. At last, it stopped after she lost her grip and found herself on the floor. The room was the same except now seven of the chairs were occupied with only the Amadeus chair empty. Tremble soon realized that she was sitting at the feet of Verina.

"You could have come and looked for us, Amadeus." Perpetua's tone was sad and pleading. "Our hearts would have been filled with joy to see you coming down the mountain."

"Unlike now, when your hearts are filled with shame."

The man that Tremble knew as Scordato stood in front of them, as if he was holding court. Tremble realized that this was the same scene she had been shown during her training. It was the time period when Scordato summoned his siblings back to the mountain for his twisted version of a reunion. It occurred to her that she thought she had seen the entire interaction. Yet, she must have seen an abbreviated version as she did not remember Baldric ever sitting down.

"Of course, we are filled with shame, brother." Baldric's response was firm and unemotional. "It was not our intent to leave our living brother here. Perpetua and I thought that you had passed. We entombed you within the Library as a place of honor for you. This was your favorite place. You could always be found surrounded by these books, Amadeus."

"Of that you are correct. This Library was my playground.

I felt safe here. That is until I was left here all alone. My name is no longer Amadeus. I am Scordato. I am the forgotten one. Meserve foretold it. It is in one of these very volumes that I shall rise from the dead by the touch of my own sister's hand."

Perpetua screamed in agony and fell to floor. Her sobs were loud and uncontrollable.

"Oh, forgive me, my darling brother. I knew not what my powers could do. I had no idea that my touch could begin to heal you." Perpetua rose up with her arms outstretched to him. "Had I known, I would have never left your side until you were well again. Oh, please forgive a young girl's ignorance. Our darling mother was not here to teach me how to use these healing hands that she passed to me."

"Oh, my dear Perpetua. It is not you who I hold responsible. Your touch was a loving goodbye to your favorite brother." Scordato turned his attention to Baldric. "It is my jealous twin who is responsible for my imprisonment here. He knew that I still had life in my veins. He is my identical; he could feel that my spirit was still with me."

"It cannot be true. Our Baldric has the kindest heart of anyone that we know."

Verina jumped up as she spoke and walked through Tremble. The young redhead momentarily stopped and looked down as if she had felt Tremble's presence. She quickly shook her head and continued to walk toward Scordato.

"You must be wrong. He would never leave someone to die. Only last year, I had the most delightful rabbit as a pet. His name was Yarnia. He had scampered out of the Land of Sojourn to visit us. I did not know that it sadden him to be away from his own family there. Baldric explained to me that over time Yarnia might die of a broken heart. Together, we took Yarnia back to

Sojourn. He is so happy now. I visit him quite often."

Tremble watched as Verina got up close to Scordato and pulled on the bottom of his jacket. Despite her small stature, even as a young child, she could hold her own in a room.

"YOU stop saying bad things about my brother. He didn't leave you behind. You were not forgotten. We have said prayers for you for as long as I can remember. My sister, Crispina, made up a song that we sang at bedtime that she calls 'Song for Amadeus.' I do not even remember you. Yet, I have missed you every day until now. I do not like you very much now. You have kept yourself away from us."

Tremble swore she saw a smile begin to cross Scordato's face. This was not the scene that she had viewed with CeCe, Bridget, Laken, and Dana. This was a different version entirely. It was as if—

Everything started moving again, faster and faster it went. Tremble felt she was sliding all over the floor. Only somehow she knew that wasn't exactly what was happening. When everything was still again, she was sitting back in Verina's chair. The paper was lying in her lap.

"It's time to go back to the Hall of Portraits. I want to go back NOW."

Chapter Ten

"THAT DID NOT take long."

Baldric was speaking to her. Tremble walked right by him. She didn't even stop to get her bearings. She was starting to feel comfortable with magic travel. She walked straight to Verina. At first, the woman looked a little apprehensive about the approach until she saw the smirk crossing Tremble's face.

"You, my dear Aunt Verina, are very devious. I like that." Tremble gave her a broad smile and a little bow. "You gave me the most valuable piece of information that anyone has yet. When all this is over, I am going to find a way to get all of you out of these dreadful frames." Tremble extended her arms and spun in a circle. She stopped as she faced Verina. "Then, you and I are going on a trip, a real live adventure."

Verina's eyes lit up with excitement. She momentarily forgot about her confinement and stood up and reached her arms out to Tremble. Realizing what she had done did not make her sad; Verina giggled like a school girl. It made Tremble's heart leap with joy.

"What are you talking about?" Again, Baldric was questioning her.

"Oh, Grand. I may not have been gone long. But, I sure did travel quite a ways."

Tremble winked at Verina before she spun around and walked toward Baldric and Perpetua. All of the sisters were framed at attention waiting to hear what she had to say.

"First of all, the book was very annoying. I had to read a whole long version of boring ancient spells. I read the entire thing and there were not any names of places, large or small, in there." Baldric started to speak. Tremble held up her hand to stop him. "That's when I started asking for help and this little pendant here provided it. Do you know anything about that, Grandmama?"

Perpetua gave Tremble a slight grin and nodded. Baldric still looked perplexed and a little aggravated.

"After that, I was able to read the book without any trouble. Strange thing was that I couldn't read anything after the point where the name appeared. I also couldn't read any of it twice. All these magical rules for different things are annoying, to say the least. I propose that we do away with some of them in the future. I believe magic should be more transparent."

Perpetua made a choking noise. This time it was Baldric who gave Tremble a little grin. She imagined that Supreme Rulers did not care much for change.

"Then, after that, I visited Amadeus' grave."

Tremble heard a half dozen muffled voices from all around her.

"You did what?" Abelia was the one who found her voice to ask the question.

"I visited Amadeus' grave. You know the box-like place in the bookcase?" Tremble paused so that they all could catch up. "And, guess what I found there?"

"That piece of paper that is following you around?"

Verina's tone was pure sarcasm. Tremble was beginning to wish that she had descended directly from that enchantress.

"That is correct. It is a message to all of you from Amadeus."

"What? You saw him? You had to encounter Scordato?" Distinct concern could be heard in Baldric's questioning.

"No, I said Amadeus. This is a note that was written to all of you while he was still Amadeus. I am certain of that. I do not know why. Yet, I am certain that is the case. Everyone listen."

Tremble heard mumblings all around her as she took a seat in front of Perpetua.

"Yes, I was left here.
Left here to die.
No one to hold my hand.
No one to cry.

Never shall you see the boy
Who you left then
The Forgotten One has gone away
But, he will return again.

Will you rejoice
And welcome him to you?
Or will you judge him
For the things he did not do?

That shall be your choice
Your burden to bear.
Some day you will have the chance
To prove that you did care."

Tremble was silent. One by one, she turned and looked at the faces of the seven siblings. All of them had expressions that could only be described as grief. No matter how many centuries had passed, the sadness they felt over the loss of their brother was still strong and painful. Perpetua and Baldric looked the worst of all of them. The weight of their grief was heavier.

"This breaks my heart all over again." Perpetua's tears flowed down her face. Tremble noticed that it made the paint run on her portrait. In a few seconds, the damage disappeared.

"It is the same sentiment we saw when we were reunited."

Tremble turned toward Abelia as she commented.

"Interesting that you are mentioning that. Our dear Verina provided me with a different view of that reunion day than I had seen before. I daresay it is a strikingly different view than many of your descendants have previously seen."

"What? I do not understand what you mean?" Baldric spoke up. "Since our physical passing, we have allowed for our exact memories to be extracted and viewed by all of our descendants as well as the legion of guardians. Even some aspects of my memory where I am not proud of my actions are crystal clear for all to see."

"I understand what you allowed. I think there has been tampering done. No, that's not true. I know there has been. It can only be one who has done it. Allow me to show you the memory of your reunion with Amadeus that I was shown while I was first learning about the Royal Family of Neverwrong."

Tremble shifted her concentration to the memory of viewing the reunion scene that was shown to her by her guardians.

"Dream stored deep in my mind, come out from where you hide."

Instantly, the image appeared in three dimensional viewing. The sisters gasped when they realized they were viewing the Library as if it was in the room with them.

Tremble stepped back and watched their reactions as the scenario played out as she had first viewed it. The segment was quite long and also included Tremble's memories of how CeCe and the others had explained different aspects to her of what she was viewing.

A rumble of whispering followed by gasps of disbelief punctuated some of the more tampered aspects of what actually occurred. Tremble could almost feel the heat of anger coming off of Baldric's painting as he saw how he was portrayed. He had been cast in the role of the arch villain who did not care at all what had happened to Amadeus.

"This is preposterous!"

Baldric got up from his chair and kicked it over within the painting. Despite all she had been told, Tremble liked him, short temper and all.

"Tremble, how did you discover this? Explain to us." Perpetua also stood up from her chair. "We need to understand."

"Sister, I can begin the explanation."

Verina's painting moved to a closer location near Perpetua and Baldric. Tremble was amazed how the portraits could shift from place to place on the circular wall. It was one aspect of the confinement that was thought out quite well.

"I cannot put my finger on what it was that Tremble said

to us earlier. The more I thought, the more it bothered me. She seemed to have the impression that we were all very flighty in our concern over Amadeus, especially Baldric." Verina paused and nodded to her brother. "As I thought about some of the other conversations we have had through the years with our descendants, I realized that same feeling is rather rampant in our family. We deserted our brother and he waged war on us."

"She is absolutely right." Gwenora spoke up. "My family has come in recent years and said that I should beg for his forgiveness. I never understood why they reacted that way. Maybe this is the answer."

"That is why I decided that the only way for us to know for sure was for Tremble to actually time travel back via my powers. I realize it was risky. I knew that Tremble would never fully understand unless she saw it for herself."

"Verina, dear, you are so wise. I am ashamed for my scolding of you when you used to take your time journeys." Perpetua reached out her hands to Verina. Her sister did the same. "It was a gift you had. You were right to use it."

"I think there is little doubt that Sebastian is behind this tampering. It probably began shortly after the actual reunion with your brother. He obviously began influencing Amadeus at a young age. He molded him into Scordato."

Tremble walked back to the center chair. All of the sisters went back to their original wall positions. Simultaneously, all of the portraits moved closer to Tremble and made a smaller circle around her.

"I do not doubt your logic, Tremble." Baldric was seated again. He was leaning in close and resting his forearms on his knees. "I am just having trouble figuring out how Sebastian was able to manipulate our memories."

"Gwenora, did you just say that your family has only brought up seeking Amadeus' forgiveness in recent years?"

"Yes, Tremble. I am sure of it. It was shortly after you were born. Everyone was talking about Jasmine's baby and how Neverwrong was going to be destroyed. My grandchildren of this generation were livid that we hadn't done anything to fix the situation in all of these centuries."

"Meserve prophesied that something would happen. It is just one big riddle though. It doesn't really talk of desolation. It says that Scordato is the forgotten one. It doesn't say who forgot him." Tremble stopped talking and let her mind wander through the collected information that she had so quickly absorbed in the early weeks of her discovering her true heritage. Then, it hit her. "Who has oversight regarding this stored heritage of your memories?"

"It is always the Supreme Ruler of Neverwrong." Perpetua answered Tremble's question. "Starting with my firstborn daughter, each Queen has been in charge of these Royal memories. They are treated as sacred."

"Who can view them?"

"Any of our descendants or the Royal Order of Guardians."

"Can they be edited or removed by the Queen?"

Tremble watched as Perpetua's eyes darted to Verina.

"Go ahead, tell her. She's already been inside my life. I am not ashamed of it."

"Verina, we were not ashamed of it either. He was a lovely man." Perpetua's voice sounded motherly. "We just did not want those generations after you to get the idea that they should all be going and doing it."

"Is this about Verina marrying a mortal?" All eyes went to Tremble. She heard a gasp or two behind her. "I think it is majorly cool. CeCe told me the story. She said that your husband was from the mortal world. He was famous and he died tragically at a young age. She said that you travelled to the future, the twentieth century, and convinced him to go back with you to Neverwrong."

"I didn't realize that my life was part of your training." Verina laughed and smiled. "I think I like that. What else did CeCe tell you? I remember her as being a very sharp young guardian."

"The feeling was definitely mutual. CeCe was intrigued by you. She told me that you learned about time travel from one of the volumes in the Library. She said that time travel was your form of rebellion. You took many trips to various eras in the human world. Your favorite was the twentieth century. That's where you found the famous mortal man of your dreams."

"And, did she reveal who he was?"

"Negative. She said that was classified information. She said that I wouldn't find a photograph of him anywhere in Neverwrong. CeCe said that he lived out his natural mortal life with you and the general citizens of Neverwrong never knew who he really was." Tremble paused and watched Verina's reaction. "So, how about telling me who this mortal celebrity was? I have a theory or two."

"Oh, Tremble, that's another story entirely. Perpetua made sure that no one in my future could learn his true identity. Like CeCe said, it's classified. The only way you could learn that is for me to send you on another time travel journey." Verina discreetly winked at Tremble. "That would be very risky."

"Tremble." Perpetua cleared her throat. "To make this long story short, the answer to your question is yes. Memories can be edited or removed by the Supreme Ruler."

"Or the designated ruler of the time?"

"What do you mean?"

"If the Supreme Ruler was not able to rule, at the time, and designated someone else to rule in her place, would that person have these editing privileges?"

"You have done it again, my dear!" Baldric's smile was broad and proud. "You have figured out another mystery. Like your father, you will make a great ruler of the Army of Neverwrong. Your abilities to dissect a situation and find the most plausible—"

"Baldric, please stop your lecture on military procedure for a moment. What are you alluding to, Tremble?" Perpetua's patience with her brother had obviously run out.

"My mother has not been able to fulfill her role as Supreme Ruler while she has been in hiding. That's twenty-one years that Belladonna has had to erase or create whatever type of memories that she would like to be credited to all of you. I've seen Belladonna in action. There's no shortage to her magical power or her powers of manipulation."

"Why would Belladonna do something so hurtful toward our family?"

It was Crispina who asked the question. She seemed to be the most reserved in disposition of all of the sisters.

"As I have been told, Belladonna was in love with a young man named Xavier."

"Oh, Xavier."

Several of the sisters said his name simultaneously. Their voices had a dreamy sound. It reminded Tremble of teenage girls talking about a handsome boy.

"As you know, Xavier was accidentally killed by Jasmine." Tremble barely got her comment out before the sisters started talking over her.

"It was such a horrendous accident."

"Could not have happened at a worse place."

"Things cannot be undone in the Garden of Mystery."

"He had such a bright future."

The sisters were talking so quickly that Tremble could not get a word in edgewise. She could see the impatience growing in Baldric.

"SISTERS!" There was silence. "Let Tremble speak."

"Thank you, Grand. As I was saying, Xavier was accidentally killed by Jasmine. Belladonna was obviously devastated. The prophecy states that the heir will reverse an act of love. Sebastian has made a deal with Belladonna that he will force me to reverse the act of love that killed Xavier."

"Belladonna believes him?"

A strange feeling came over Tremble. It was a sick feeling in the pit of her stomach as she realized that she might have said too much in their present location.

"Oh, my darling girl, do not worry." Perpetua's soothing voice pulled Tremble out of her deep thought. "We have put a shield around us for this entire conversation—the previous one and now."

"What a relief! I am still not used to all these magical ways of surveillance that enchanters use. I keep forgetting to think about those things before I speak." Tremble paused and let out a huge sigh. "Can all of you read my mind?"

"No, my dear." Abelia answered. "Only Perpetua and Baldric can because you are their descendant. I have no doubt, though, that we can all read your heart. It is pure and resolute in its determination to overcome all that is attacking us."

"I thank you for that vote of confidence, Abelia. I sure do hope that I have the opportunity to get to know each one of you when we are on the other side of this horrid situation."

"Until then, Tremble, let's go back to talking about this influence you think Sebastian is exercising over Belladonna." Baldric stood up within his frame and walked to the edge. "If he influenced her to manipulate our memories of certain situations, I would imagine that he did the same with Amadeus. Do you think that he has enough collective power that he is able to reverse what Amadeus once knew as truth?"

"In the mortal world, there is a psychological phenomenon called the Stockholm Syndrome. It is a state of bonding that sometimes can occur in which a hostage develops empathy, sympathy, and even positive feelings toward his or her captors. It can even go as far as the hostage defending and identifying with the captor. The longer that they are together, the tighter the bond can become. I think in an advanced stage, the hostage would believe whatever the captor said." Tremble paused to allow for what she had said to sink in with her audience.

"Think of the centuries that Sebastian has cast his influence over Amadeus and molded him into Scordato. I'm sure that Scordato considers him to be his ally now. He let the word 'mentor' slip when I last saw him. I know for a fact that he does not even think that he is being influenced by anyone. I am also sure that he does not think that Sebastian is The Evil that took your parents. It is beyond his current comprehension that Sebastian and The Evil could be one."

"This is worse than we ever imagined." Perpetua rose and stood at the edge of her frame. She and Baldric looked as if they were standing side by side. "We must do everything in our power to help Tremble fight Sebastian and destroy him."

"She cannot do it alone." Baldric's voice was loud and bold. "She will have to have as many allies as possible."

Baldric exchanged a glance with Perpetua. Tremble wondered if they were communicating.

"Tremble, my dear, Baldric, my sisters and I need to discuss something. Would you be so kind as to leave us alone for a little while?"

"Certainly, Grandmama. Where should I go?"

"Momentarily, a door will appear and open for you. It will lead to a room where a lovely meal has been prepared for you. I'm sure that you must be famished."

"Now that you mention it, I am hungry. Do you think I might also be able to communicate with my mother?"

"I think that is a lovely idea. I would ask that you wait until you return to us. I would like to speak with Jasmine, also."

As Perpetua finished speaking, the portraits moved out of their tight circle. Baldric's moved out of the way. Just as Perpetua said, a door appeared and opened for her. Tremble gave them a smile and walked into the bright room.

Chapter Eleven

Upon entering the room, Tremble was perplexed at first. The floor, ceiling, and walls were entirely white, bright white. In a few seconds, her eyes began to adjust to the lack of color and she could see that there was a long white table in the center of the room as well as a comfortable looking white chair.

Everything changed when Tremble sat down. Beautiful colors filled the room as if an artist was painting. She smiled as she watched the walls come to life with wallpaper and décor. On the floor, a large Persian rug with deep rich colors appeared. The table became a mahogany color and was also immediately filled with a buffet of succulent looking dishes, breads, fruits, and vegetables.

Tremble strained from her now purple velvet and mahogany chair to see the far end of the table. Her mouth watered as decadent desserts became visible including cakes that were over two feet tall and a fountain of luscious dark chocolate.

It did not take her long to dig into the foods that were closest to her. After taking a few delicious bites, she realized that she was indeed starving. Barely stopping long enough to chew, Tremble consumed more food than she ought to have in such a short time. She was so caught up in eating that she did not notice that she was not alone.

Tremble had to lean over the right arm of her chair to see the person. It appeared to be a little girl and she was hidden behind one of the very large cakes.

"Hello."

A tiny face quickly bobbed in Tremble's direction and hid behind the cake again.

"My name is Tremble. What's your name?"

Tremble heard a little whisper of a voice.

"Oh, I didn't hear you. Could you come a little closer?"

The little girl peeked out again. This time, Tremble was able to see that she had a short pixie cut of ebony hair. Long, dark eyelashes framed jade green eyes. Her petite face looked like that of a porcelain doll. She was beautiful.

Tremble gave the little one her biggest smile and a wink. She picked up a large heart shaped cookie that was on a plate closer to her and held it out as a lure. She could tell that the child was pondering her next move.

"Well, if you don't want it, I guess I will have to eat it."

Tremble pretended that she was going to take a big bite out of the cookie. Before, she knew what was happening the little girl flew to Tremble's chair and snatched the cookie from her grasp. The child hovered just above and to the right side of Tremble as she took a delicate little bite.

In a matter of a few seconds, the large cookie had disappeared. The girl flew around the room as if she was on a sugar high.

"My name is Cinnamon." The voice was still soft, but stronger. "You are the Queen's daughter."

The little girl's statement surprised Tremble. She paused and watched as the child's wings rapidly fluttered to keep her hovering in one spot.

"Nice to meet you, Cinnamon. Yes, my mother is Jasmine. Do you know her?"

"Oh, yes, we all know about Queen Jasmine. I have never seen her. They all say she is very beautiful."

"Yes, I do believe she is. She has been in hiding for a very long time."

"She has been gone for your whole life. You are the hidden one."

Tremble thought to herself that was another name given her that she could do without.

"What is your role here in Neverwrong?"

Tremble waved her hand and another chair appeared that was closer to her. She motioned for Cinnamon to sit down. At first, the girl hesitated. But, when Tremble put a plate of fruit down at the setting, Cinnamon flew to the chair and sat down. Her tiny hands reached out and snatched a piece. Her movements were so fast, Tremble's eyes could not keep up.

"Well, mostly, I am a little girl." Cinnamon giggled and snatched another strawberry that was almost as big as her hand.

"Are you an enchantress?"

"No, I can do some magic. I will learn more when I grow up. My people are wizlets."

"I'm afraid I don't know what that means."

"We are magical like a wizard, but we can fly like fairies. In the Kingdom of Neverwrong, lots of us take care of the animals in the Land of Sojourn. We help the enchanters in different ways. My mother was a helper to Queen Jasmine when she healed people. I am training to be a secret keeper."

"A secret keeper? That sounds like a very important job."

"Oh, it is." Cinnamon's beautiful eyes grew wide and her expression turned serious. "Her Royal Highness says that I will be the best secret keeper ever. I already have many of hers that I am keeping tightly guarded."

"Are you speaking of Belladonna?"

"Oh, yes, Her Royal Highness." Cinnamon bowed her head.

"Belladonna is my aunt."

"Yes, she is Queen Jasmine's sister."

"I bet that Belladonna has lots of secrets about Queen Jasmine." Tremble wondered how much this little girl would divulge.

"Oh yes, I know many of them. I know secrets about you, too."

Cinnamon giggled as she took a big bite out of a green grape. Tremble caught a glimpse of the child's tiny, perfectly shaped teeth. Instead of being white, they were an iridescent shade of pink.

"You know secrets about me? Oh my, that's not fair. I should know my own secrets."

Tremble watched as Cinnamon stopped chewing and pondered what she had said. The little girl's expressions were adorable. As Cinnamon thought about Tremble's reply, she scrunched her nose and wiggled it like a rabbit. Tremble looked closely at her face to make sure there weren't whiskers under her nose.

"Her Royal Highness says that I am not supposed to share any of the secrets." Cinnamon took a deep breath and set the grape down. She crossed her arms with a look of deviance. "But, she didn't tell me what I should do if I ever met you. Maybe I should go ask her."

Cinnamon fluttered up from the table. Tremble could see that except for the wings and her tiny size, she looked like a normal little girl.

"Oh no, that's not necessary. I have a secret for you to keep, too."

"A secret of yours for me to keep? Oh, I am so excited!" Cinnamon sat back down in the chair. "I am a really good secret keeper. Everyone says so."

"I can tell." Tremble shook her head and smiled. "You are the best secret keeper I have ever met." Tremble almost rolled her eyes at her own sarcasm. "My secret is going to be hard for you. This will be a real challenge. I cannot tell you unless you promise not to tell Belladonna."

"That is hard. I am supposed to tell Belladonna everything that I see and hear."

This time, Tremble did roll her eyes. Cinnamon was Belladonna's personal spy. Sly one indeed to make a sweet looking little wizard girl as an informant.

"I understand that you have your orders. You do realize that I will be Queen one day?"

"Oh, that's not going to happen." Cinnamon's eyes grew big as she realized what she said. Her little hands covered her mouth. "I didn't say that."

"What? I didn't catch what you said." Tremble faked not hearing.

"I just said, yes I know. You are going to be Queen someday. I am a really good secret keeper. Please tell me your secret."

"I'm not sure. I've just met you. How do I know that I can

trust you?"

"Oh, you can! You can!" Cinnamon stood up in the chair. "I'm very trustable."

"I think you will have to prove it to me."

Tremble pushed her chair back from the table and stood up. "How can I do that?"

"Well, it would have to be something very important. I think I could trust you if you told me one of the secrets you knew about me." Cinnamon closed her mouth tightly and shook her head. "I mean, after all, it is about me. It's not really telling if the secret is about the person you tell it to."

Cinnamon gave Tremble a concentrated look. She appeared to be seriously pondering what Tremble had said. Instead of flying, the little girl climbed down from her own chair and stood facing Tremble.

"You wouldn't tell Her Royal Highness that I told you?"

"Absolutely not."

"Pinky swear." Cinnamon held out the pinky of her right hand.

"Pinky swear." Tremble locked her pinky finger with Cinnamon's. She felt a burst of magic pass between them.

"You are very powerful." Cinnamon's eyes grew big again. "Laken said you would be. I didn't believe him."

"You know Laken, too. He's my best friend." Tremble didn't realize how she felt until the words were out of her mouth.

"He's so dreamy. I want to marry him." Cinnamon fluttered her long eyelashes and blushed a little. "He loved you though, even before he met you."

Tremble felt a lump form in her throat. She couldn't let Cinnamon see that something was wrong. Taking a deep breath, she turned around and pretended to stretch.

"Oh, I just bet that he loves you, too."

"Do you think so?" Cinnamon scurried around to face Tremble as she was wiping her eyes. "What's the matter? Did I make you sad?"

"Oh no, my dear." Tremble kneeled down to be eye level with the girl. "I am just very tired. Eating all that wonderful food made me sleepy and that made my eyes cry."

"Okay, I understand." Cinnamon paused and reached to touch Tremble's hair. "I love the purple streaks in your hair. I wish I had some."

Tremble was not sure where the knowledge came from, yet, within in her mind she heard the words to a spell.

"Ebony locks, beautiful shine, give my Cinnamon some purple like mine."

Tremble ran her fingers over Cinnamon's hair and instantly purple highlights glistened all through the black. Tremble waved her hand and a large round mirror appeared. She turned it around so that Cinnamon could see her reflection.

"Weeee! I love it!"

The little girl squealed with delight. She pulled Tremble into a big hug and gently kissed her on the cheek. For a split second, Tremble saw, what she thought was a vision of something from the little girl's life. Belladonna stood over Cinnamon. She was very angry looking and was yelling at the girl. Around Belladonna's neck was the red diamond pendant that Tremble had seen before. Belladonna was holding the pendant in her hand and rubbing it. Cinnamon let go of Tremble and the vision stopped.

"I am sorry. Did I do something wrong?"

Tremble made her mind come back to the present and looked at Cinnamon. The child looked afraid and sad.

"Oh no, my dear. Everything is fine. That was a very nice

hug. I needed it." Tremble gently touched Cinnamon's hair. "I'm glad that you like your hair. We are twins now. Isn't that fun?"

Cinnamon nodded her head in agreement as she scampered back over to the mirror. She made several different little poses to look at her hair.

Tremble hadn't paid much attention to what the child was wearing. Her dress was cute, but plain. After a little thought about what she would like to see, Tremble snapped her fingers and Cinnamon's dress changed to a beautiful lavender with tiny butterflies. Cinnamon gasped and jumped up and down in delight.

"I know that you do not need to have to explain where the dress came from or how your hair changed. So, this is going to be our little secret." Tremble waved her hands up and down over Cinnamon's hair and body. "Mirror mirror, let it be, only beauty we can see. From the eyes of others hide, Cinnamon's secret deep inside."

Cinnamon squealed again as she looked in the mirror. The reflected image was just as she had originally been. Yet, when she looked down at herself, the child could see the pretty lavender dress.

"Oh, you are very powerful. I think I can trust you with your secrets."

"I am so glad that I have earned your trust."

"Her Royal Highness says that you are going to bring her love back to her. She says that you will not be happy about it, but you will do it so that you can save your mother."

"Queen Jasmine?"

"No, your other mother, the one who hid you in the other world."

A feeling of fear instantly came over Tremble. It had not

occurred to her that Belladonna or anyone else would use Dana as a pawn to get her to do things.

"What else does she say about me?"

"She says that you will never be the Queen of Neverwrong because there will soon be a new King, and Her Royal Highness and her love will help him rule the kingdom." Cinnamon bowed her head. "She said that I could be the highest secret keeper when that happened." Cinnamon looked around and her voice was just a whisper. "I don't trust her though. She tells people different versions of things. My mother says that the truth does not have versions."

"Your mother is very wise. Where is she? Where is your family?"

"They are all in the Land of Sojourn, with the animals. My mother is an animal healer like Queen Jasmine heals people."

"Why aren't you with them?" Tremble took hold of Cinnamon's little hand as she had begun to look sad.

"I have to work for Her Royal Highness."

"You are so young. You should be with your family."

"I am a little like you, Princess Tremble."

Tremble momentarily thought of Laken and her chastising him for using the same title.

"I have extra special powers. I can see into beings and tell if they are good or evil."

"Really? That is a very special power. What do you see when you look into me?"

"You are very good. So is Laken. Most enchanters and enchantresses in our kingdom are very good. Some have a little evil, but not too much." Cinnamon giggled.

"What about Belladonna?"

"Her Royal Highness is good, most of the time. Except

when she holds her amulet."

"What do you mean?"

"She has a big red diamond that hangs on a long chain around her neck. The necklace belongs to Queen Jasmine. Her Royal Highness is keeping it for her while she is away. It originally belonged to Her Royal Highness Claudia. She is the original mother of all of Neverwrong."

Cinnamon stretched out her arms all around her as if she was showing Tremble a large place. The action made Tremble smile at the simplicity of her description.

"So what happens when Belladonna holds the amulet?"

"I see darkness in her heart." Cinnamon shook like a chill had come over her. "Her Royal Highness says that it was infused with power by the man who will become the King of Neverwrong. She says it is her source of power." Cinnamon covered her mouth again.

"What's wrong, little one?" Tremble pulled her into a hug as the child had begun to shake all over. "Everything is okay. Do not be afraid."

"I told a secret that was not about you. Her Royal Highness will lock me away in the Garden of Stone." Cinnamon paused and looked behind her before she began whispering. "I have never been there, but I have heard it is very scary. There are people there who are made of stone."

Tremble sighed as she thought about the two brave young men who were now made of stone all because of their love for her. She swallowed the lump that formed again in her throat.

"Belladonna will never know that you told me. It's still a secret."

"Her Royal Highness is not evil on her own. That amulet can make her act very scary."

Suddenly, everything in the room began to disappear as the room turned back to solid white.

"Oh my!" Cinnamon began to look afraid as everything was disappearing.

"It is fine. I think you better go though." Tremble stopped as a thought hit her. "How did you get in here anyway?"

Cinnamon did not have to answer as Tremble saw for herself. The little girl faded away just like everything else did. Before she completely disappeared, the child blew Tremble a kiss and she was gone.

Tremble stood in awe in the again solid white room.

"Was any of that real?"

As she asked the question, a door appeared and opened. Tremble lingered for a few minutes as she stared at the white walls, floor, and ceiling. There was a fine line between fantasy and reality in the world she found herself. As Tremble walked back into the Hall of Portraits, she wondered if she might be walking back into another illusion.

"DID YOU ENJOY your meal, Tremble?"

All of the portraits were in their assigned spots when Tremble re-entered the room.

"It was very delicious, Abelia. I also enjoyed the entertainment."

Tremble watched their reactions. Each of them looked surprised or confused.

"I do not understand what you mean." Perpetua verbalized what all of them seemed to be thinking.

"Who worked the magic for the beautiful room and the table

of food?"

"I did." Perpetua looked even more perplexed. "I chose what I hoped would be a lovely selection of different—"

"The food was awesome. I ate too much of it. What I want to know is who created the little girl who came and joined me?"

"What little girl? Someone came into the room? It was protected by a spell."

Tremble sat down in her chair. She shook her head as her mind raced to remember any clues that might help determine how the child had gotten there.

"There was a little girl who came into the room after I first arrived. She said that her name was Cinnamon and that she was a wizlet."

"A wizlet? You don't say! All of the wizlets live in Sojourn, don't they, Baldric?" Verina had moved herself to a position closer to Tremble.

"That is what I thought. Of course, it has been eons since I was involved in any of the oversight of Sojourn or any of the other villages."

"Wizlets are real? This wasn't some illusion someone created?"

"Yes, wizlets are very real. They have special powers. One of them, I cannot remember her name, trained with Jasmine. She was a healer. She heals the animals now."

Abelia stood up in her portrait and changed the view behind her to what Tremble remembered to be the Land of Sojourn. There were many different types of animals wandering around. A small woman in a white coat was doctoring what appeared to be a lion. The woman turned toward them and Tremble saw an older version of the sweet face that had been her meal companion.

"That's Cinnamon's mother. It has to be."

"I just cannot imagine how a wizlet got in that room." Perpetua was pacing within her frame.

"Did you include sweets in the menu, sister?"

Tremble laughed as she saw that Crispina raised her hand as she asked her question.

"Yes, I did. Oh my, that is it. Wizlets have the power to latch on to a spell, and sugar is the component that binds them. Crispina, you are so wise with these types of details." Perpetua stopped pacing and gave her sister a hearty smile. "Tremble, I am so sorry for the interruption of your meal. I hope the wizlet was not a nuisance to your relaxation and—"

"Cinnamon was not a nuisance. She was a delightful child. A child who works for Belladonna."

"WHAT?" Baldric could not contain his shock or dislike.

"Cinnamon said she was a secret keeper for Her Royal Highness. She said 'Her Royal Highness' about a dozen times or more. Basically, my take on the situation is that Cinnamon is a spy. She is supposed to tell Belladonna everything she sees or hears. She has to be very young. She has been separated from her family because she has this special gift."

"What is this gift? Wizlets have a variety of special gifts." Abelia had retrieved a book from a shelf within her area and was quickly flipping through it.

"Cinnamon said that she had the ability to see within a being and determine whether they were good or evil."

"That is quite rare." Abelia looked up from the book. "It is a power that would make her an excellent spy. She could learn things from just being in the presence of someone."

"Tremble, do you think she was spying on you?" Perpetua seemed in awe of the situation.

"Actually, I do not think so. If you say that she could get into your spell because of the sugar, as outlandish as that sounds to me, I think it might have truly been a little girl following her craving. She seemed surprised to see me and a little frightened at the beginning. I cannot imagine that she was lying to me."

"Absolutely not." Abelia held up a book and pointed to a passage. "It says here that wizlets who have the Power of Perception do not have the ability to lie. It is impossible for them to do so."

"Tremble, we have much to discuss with you." Baldric seemed to have calmed down. "But, first, I think that you should tell us, in detail, what transpired between you and this wizlet child. I think there is more to this than what you may have detected."

A half an hour later, Tremble had finished recounting her time within the white room with Cinnamon. Several of the sisters had detailed questions about the wizlet child. Baldric's expression during the discussion could be best described as dark concern. Tremble thought that her grandfather was like a smoldering storm that was going to burst on the horizon. She could not imagine what he would do if he was out of the frame. His physical life as a warrior must have been legendary.

"I tend to agree with Tremble." Abelia was the first one to voice her opinion. "It is not in a wizlet's nature to be deceptive. I think that if she had been sent by Belladonna to spy, Cinnamon would have shown that in her expressions. Wizlets are astute at reading others. They are not good at hiding their own motives or emotions. You might call them an open book in that regard."

"It is very possible that Cinnamon was drawn to Tremble." Perpetua nodded her head in agreement as she explained her thoughts. "The child obviously possesses great power. She has exceptional abilities to read into others. Tremble's power would be like a magnet to her. The sugar might have just been the link to what she was already trying to find."

"My concerns are not with the motives of the child." Baldric had been out of the normal view of his frame for a few moments. "What we do not know is how this child will be manipulated into telling about her encounter with Tremble."

"How does that matter? I did not tell her anything."

"It matters because Belladonna will then know that you are aware of her darker motives." Baldric sat down in his chair. "It also matters because of what might happen to that sweet child."

Tremble's eyes began filling with tears as she thought about the sweet little being who she had just given purple streaks in her pixie hair.

"If Cinnamon came into this room, would she be protected here?"

"Oh, most certainly, the protection around this chamber is from our own combined magic. One thing that Scordato could not take away from us. We are much stronger than him." Baldric's expression showed strength and conviction.

"I want Cinnamon the Wizlet to be here in this room!"

Before Tremble could look around at anyone's reaction, the little girl she had just met appeared in front of her. Cinnamon immediately looked terrified as she saw the faces in the portraits looking down at her.

"Cinnamon, it's okay. I'm here."

The child whirled around and ran into Tremble's arms. Cinnamon was shaking uncontrollably and crying.

"How? How did I get it here?"

Tremble kneeled down and wiped the tears that were flowing down Cinnamon's cheek.

"I wished for you to be here and now it is so."

"Oh, you are so powerful, Princess Tremble. Why did you wish for me?"

Cinnamon seemed to momentarily forget that there was an audience surrounding her. The child's attention was focused on Tremble. Her tiny hand touched Tremble's face so gently that it was like a feather falling.

"You do not need to call me Princess, little one. I am just Tremble." She watched as Cinnamon stared up at her. The beautiful tiny lashes that framed her sparkling eyes fluttered rapidly. "I thought you might be safer if you were here with me instead of being a spy. With the help of these fine ladies and gentleman who you see all around you, I am going to protect you and keep you safe."

Cinnamon took her gaze off of Tremble and began to look at each of the portraits. The occupants smiled down on her. She was careful not to leave Tremble's grasp even as she moved to look around the circle.

"Those are the original ones." Cinnamon whispered and pointed. "They are the great ones who built Neverwrong. They shared their power with those who had none and loved the people and animals who had wandered to this land."

Tremble was awestruck by the child's knowledge. Cinnamon had great wisdom and understanding of the magical world she lived in. Perpetua and the others nodded and smiled at her.

"Is it okay that I brought you here?"

Cinnamon stood up and began to walk around the circle. She stopped at each portrait for a moment. She did not say a word before she moved on to the next one. When she found her way back to Tremble, she began to speak.

"You are going to fight a great battle. It will be dangerous. Not everyone will survive. Someone you love will perish. It is the way it is." Cinnamon looked back to those who were around her. "These are your family. They are very brave. They will help you. It is their power that shall be the force behind you. I will help you, too."

Tremble was startled as Perpetua and the others began clapping their hands. The action caused Cinnamon to blush and beam with pride. She twirled around the room as her wings carried her to each portrait.

"Can they see my pretty dress and the purple in my hair?"

Tremble snapped her fingers as Cinnamon asked her question.

"We most certainly can, Cinnamon." Abelia raised her clapping hands above her head. "Bravo! You look lovely. You look like our dear Tremble."

Her tiny wings fluttered with great speed as she excitedly flew around the room. As she zoomed by Tremble, she barely missed her head.

"Cinnamon, we need for you to settle down now." Perpetua tried to get Cinnamon's attention. "We have many things to tell Tremble."

Cinnamon did not waste any time following the direction. She landed near the frame of Verina. A chair, just her size, appeared in front of the portrait. Cinnamon smiled and sat down.

"Tremble, we have been discussing what we can do to help you." Baldric began the discussion. "It is obvious to us that when you leave this room, you will no doubt be forced to face The Evil, in its many forms."

"Yes, but I also must find a way to free Laken and Jake from their current state."

"Oh, oh, what's happened to Laken? I love Laken." Cinnamon covered her mouth. "Sorry."

"Cinnamon, I did not want to tell you before. I knew it would upset you. Since you are now here with us, I suppose that I can no longer hide the truth from you. Laken has been imprisoned in stone, like Claudia and Marcellus." The little girl gasped. "My friend. Jake, from the mortal world, has also been imprisoned this same way."

"May I speak?"

"Certainly, our little friend." Baldric's kind tone to Cinnamon somewhat shocked Tremble. He seemed quite smitten with the child.

"I know about this. I know it from my secrets. I am bound to my bonds of secrecy."

Cinnamon paused and tapped her head with her tiny hand. Tremble smiled to herself as the child looked like she was hoping to wake up a thought that was hidden in her head.

"Secrets that I hold within are forbidden for me to speak. My vow did not extend to showing you." A huge smile crossed her face. "May I?"

"Most certainly!"

Perpetua replied as Cinnamon flew up into the air. The tiny being was chanting to herself and doing little flips in the air as she did so. Tremble was so caught up in watching the child's acrobatics that she failed to notice what was actually happening around her.

"Tremble, pay attention!"

Baldric's barking voice made Tremble jump. As she did, she looked around. Their view had changed dramatically. The portraits had quickly moved to a cluster on one side of the room as the opposite side became what looked like a beautiful terraced garden. Tremble saw two people in the distant corner. She could see a partial view of Cinnamon sitting on a small chair close to the edge of the view. Tremble looked around her. Cinnamon was hovering in the air in the corner behind her. She was seeing one of Cinnamon's memories. The little girl smiled in delight and pointed to the view. The two people walked closer and Tremble could see that it was Belladonna and a man.

"Oh, Baldric, I will never forget that face, that is—"

"Don't say the name we knew, sister. He was Sebastian when our father first befriended him." Baldric took a deep breath. "I know that what we are about to hear is going to be painful. Here is our descendant, this beautiful girl, who has let The Evil take control of her."

Baldric grew silent as they could see that Belladonna had begun talking.

"You must tell me again how you will do it. It cannot be painful. I will not have you torture this child. Despite the loathing that I feel for the actions of her mother, I do not hold the child responsible."

"Why do you let your pretty head fret over this? Long or short, easy or hard, you want what the child can do. She is the only one who can bring back what was taken from you."

The voice was very familiar to Tremble. She had heard it for what seemed like hours in the Garden of Stone. She was anxious to see the face that went with it, to see if he was still the beautiful being who had won young Inezia's love or if he was as horrid looking as his actions. He had not turned into their view.

"Oh, how I long to see Xavier again. Our lives shall be wonderful. You will find him very useful in the work you have planned. He is a valiant warrior." Belladonna clutched the red diamond tightly in her hand.

"He *was* a valiant warrior. I will be the one who undoes that action. I shall make the heir reverse an act of love. Tremble shall indeed live up to her name as she feels my power."

"Again, I do not want to hear such talk. At some point, I may have to face my grieving sister. I do not want to know what you do to Tremble."

"Beautiful Belladonna, you can be so naïve. The only place you may face Jasmine might be if she is foolish enough to try to save her daughter. I shall dispose of her and Forrest with much haste after Tremble has delivered your love to you."

"I did not realize you had that intent." For a moment, Tremble heard concern in Belladonna's voice. The moment passed quickly. "I suppose it is only logical that they must be out of the picture so that your transition to reign shall be easier."

At that moment, Sebastian turned and faced them. There were gasps from the younger sisters in the room. Tremble herself almost choked on her own saliva as she saw the face of The Evil, once and for all.

Chapter Twelve

HAT DOES EVIL look like? Tremble froze the image of Sebastian in her mind. In her mortal upbringing, she had learned to accept the face of evil as something ugly or grotesque. Whether it was actually true or not, history portrayed devils as being hideous and frightening. She remembered hearing her parents have a long discussion once about the topic. Her father had a very different view. He said that there was no reason to believe that evil was necessarily ugly. Evil would be the most alluring and, thus, successful, if it was actually a beauty that was rare and striking.

Andrew's theory was confirmed right before Tremble's eyes. The face of Sebastian was breathtaking. So handsome were his features that he did not look real. Dark chocolate brown hair hung in soft waves that framed his face and barely touched the collar of his jacket. Tremble could see dark eyes hidden behind long lashes and perfect eyebrows. His chiseled face could have easily found a home on the pages of the world's most famous magazines with his clear soft tan complexion.

The face of The Evil was beautiful, and it was looking straight at Tremble smiling like a hungry dog. She was surprised that her spine was not frozen as the chill that was going down it felt like a thick icicle falling down her back.

"He looks like he can see us."

Tremble's words were a whisper that everyone heard.

"It is part of his charm. He has a way about him that draws you in. Poor Inezia never stood a chance. Our father and mother believed that he was just a handsome stranger."

Perpetua's words were laced with a tone of sadness. As Tremble glanced in the direction of her and Baldric, she saw that they both had a look of defeat. The past was haunting them in more ways than one.

"He is very bad. There is no good in him. Absolutely, positively, not even a smidgen."

Cinnamon's sudden comment caused everyone to look in her direction. She was no longer hovering in the corner. Somehow, the tiny wizlet had joined Perpetua within her frame. She was holding her hand. From the look on Perpetua's face, Tremble wasn't sure if she had realized until Cinnamon spoke that she was there with her.

"How did—" All Tremble could get out was a couple of words as she pointed at the portrait in shock.

"Wizlet's are very powerful creatures in strange little ways." Abelia responded as Cinnamon jumped over into her frame. She gave the girl a firm hug. "We do not know the capacity of their magic as it can suddenly change for seemingly no reason. Little Cinnamon might be able to enter our framed world today, tomorrow she might not have the ability."

"My mother says our magic comes as we need it."

Cinnamon giggled and jumped out of Abelia's frame and back to Tremble. She pointed at Sebastian.

"Bad man, be gone!"

Cinnamon snapped her fingers and the view disappeared. Everyone began moving back to their usual positions.

"Why did you show us that?" Tremble gave the girl a hug and stroked her hair.

"He plans to kill you and your parents. He really wants everyone gone. Her Royal Highness has been evilly tricked. He will not return her love."

"So, he does not intend for me to reverse an act of love?"

"Oh, yes, he has plans for you to do that very thing. He mumbles to himself about it constantly. But, it is not the act of love for which he wants to use your power. He wants that all for himself."

"Child, tell us more." Baldric's voice was calm, but commanding. "Do not be afraid. You are within the safety of our power now."

"I am not afraid. My heart would never heal if my silence helped him carry out all he has planned. My mother could not heal me if I played a role in all this evil." Cinnamon bowed her head and took a very deep breath. "He wants you to bring back his child."

"What? I don't understand. Inezia said that *Sebastian* killed their child."

"He mumbles. I am not sure that I understand all that he says. He speaks of his son, his precious son. That it was not the right time for him to be born. He had to take that life so that he could give him a life of power."

"What do you two know of this?" Tremble turned to Perpetua and Baldric. "Surely, you must have heard the child mentioned as you were older."

"We were babes ourselves. It was not spoken about. After we came to this land, our parents were gone all too soon and Inezia disappeared." Baldric's answer was direct, but he looked as if he was somewhere far away.

"I have never spoken about this. My young mind could not understand it. My older mind has not wanted to remember." Perpetua looked at Baldric as she spoke. An expression of surprise crossed his face. "After we fled The Evil in our homeland, when things had settled down some, I overhead our mother comforting Inezia. Our dear caretaker was beside herself with grief. She was sobbing with sadness. Our mother's gentle voice and healing spirit was comforting her friend. I was supposed to be asleep on a bed nearby." Perpetua looked at Tremble and smiled.

"Children rarely sleep when they are told to do so. I knew that if I was very still and kept my eyes closed they would keep talking. My curious spirit did not realize that I would hear the unimaginable." Perpetua made eye contact with her sisters. It seemed to strengthen her. "Part of Inezia's source of grief was that she was never able to see her son, to hold him. When a woman carries a child to term and gives birth to that child, she expects to hold it in her arms."

Tremble watched as Perpetua looked at Gwenora with a look of sorrow.

"Do not burden your heart with this again, Perpetua. It was not your fault. It is not your cross to bear. I have long ago made my peace with what happened." Gwenora looked at Tremble. "If you have not been told, I was the first one of my siblings to pass. I died while giving birth and was robbed of the chance to hold my child. My heart hurts more for Inezia than myself. Yet, I have been able to know that child just as I now know you, my dear."

Tremble had forgotten that Gwenora never held her child. How strange it must have been to be able to see your child grow from the confines of a frame, yet, never be able to reach out and hold his hand.

"You are strong, my sister. You could have been a great comfort to our Inezia. I digress with my story." Perpetua dabbed her eyes with a hankie she had tucked in her sleeve and cleared her throat. "Inezia knew, with the exception of Sebastian, there had been only one other person in the room when her child was born. It was our mother. Being a healer, Claudia had insisted that since the child was coming so early, she needed to be there to help in any way possible. Inezia had confided her fears about the baby to her sister-in-law, her closest friend. Fears of what the child would be like as she felt it growing so fast and large inside of her. What had been the blindness of her love for Sebastian became the reality that she did not know who or what she had married."

Tremble glanced at Cinnamon. The child had settled into a slightly hidden spot between two of the portraits. She seemed spellbound by Perpetua's story and at the same time nodding in agreement as if she knew how it was going to end.

"I understood from Inezia's words that she had beseeched our mother previously to tell her about the child—a son. For some reason on that day, Mother decided it was time to tell her what she wanted to know. I cannot say that I remember it all, word for word. Some of it made no sense to me, so I did not retain it. I suppose I could call the memory forth. I do not think the detail would enhance the telling of the story. As I have thought about it in my adulthood, I have reasoned that our mother decided that it was better for Inezia to know the truth than to believe her own imagination."

"Our mother was so gentle and kind." Baldric suddenly spoke. "You sisters have her manner. All of you have her kindness and wisdom."

"Inezia knew that the child was quite large, unusually so for the number of months that she had been carrying him. Our mother used her healing skills to ease the pain that would have no doubt come from birthing such a large baby. She told Inezia that the child was not deformed, in the sense that many might think. The child was advanced in age. She said he looked like a toddler as he came out and quickly became older looking as the next few minutes passed. Something about this process was what horrified Sebastian."

"What in the world could this mean? Do you know of any beings who age so quickly?" Tremble searched her brain for any knowledge, quickly realizing that any she might have would only apply to the mortal world.

"It was not just the aging that Mother noticed. He also grew in size. The more this happened, the angrier Sebastian became. Before she realized what was happening, Sebastian had picked the child up and carried him out of the room. The child was never seen again."

"Does anyone know what Sebastian did with him?"

Perpetua nodded negatively, so did Baldric.

"I know." The little hidden voice answered. "He took him to the one they call Meserve."

"Back to Meserve again. Everything seems to rotate back to him eventually."

"Tremble, he was our grandfather. He was the most powerful enchanter to have ever lived."

"He *is* your grandfather. Despite his incredible age, he is still very much alive."

Baldric rubbed his forehead and sighed. The younger sisters whispered to each other. Tremble caught a glimpse of Cinnamon. The child looked a little confused.

"It is not a surprise to hear this. Meserve is the source of all our power. We knew that his heart was still beating. That does not always mean that a being is still alive." Baldric's words were solemn. "Only he knows what happened to that child. He never would reveal it. We have not seen him for a hundred years or more."

"It is not the time for us to be concerned about Meserve." Perpetua took control of the discussion. "Before the arrival of this little one, we were about to talk with Tremble about what we have done during her absence. We must continue."

"I am very intent on hearing what you have planned. There is no time to waste. I am very concerned about Laken, Jake, and Forrest." Tremble leaned closer to the portrait of her grandmother.

"What? Is there something more about Forrest that you have not told us?"

"Sebastian bombarded me with so much information. It's hard to keep it all straight. I daresay that I do not even grasp what he has done to my father. He told me that he splintered his power. Sebastian mockingly chided my father's name and said that he was now 'the Forrest in the trees.' I think he has done something to break Forrest's power into different parts."

"Perpetua, do you think what Tremble is referring to might be zippling?"

Tremble was startled to hear the voice of Elsavetta. The enchantress had been relatively quiet throughout both of Tremble's visits to the room.

"Oh, Elsavetta, I believe you might be correct."

"Zippling? That must be another term that I did not learn in my speed course in enchanting."

"Tremble, it will take you your current lifetime times five to touch the surface of the vast knowledge pertaining to magic." Abelia had retrieved several other books, from what Tremble could only imagine was a massive library. "Zippling is old magic. It is not commonplace in the present time. I would daresay that only a few of our grandchildren have even heard the term. It most certainly was something that Sebastian learned at the feet of Meserve."

"It does seem that Meserve was quite generous with his knowledge. That would seem to be contradictory to the wisdom that you all claim he has."

"Tremble, I would not go so far as to make that judgment." Baldric walked to the edge of his frame and stared at Tremble. "Before The Evil invaded our existence, the magical world was relatively peaceful. As our father, the great Marcellus, would recount, a flared temper or an accident might be more likely to cause conflict than the outright plotting of dissension among neighboring kingdoms. He learned, from his father Meserve, how to maintain peace instead of how to wage war."

"It is truth that our brother speaks. If Sebastian was a willing learner, Meserve, no doubt, enjoyed recounting the ancient spells." Elsavetta again spoke about the topic. "Zippling is a rather complicated magic process that none of us in this room have ever performed. I do not think his borrowed power would allow him to perform this alone. Sebastian had to have help."

"Help that Scordato might surely have provided." Baldric's tone turned dark.

"We must not forget Belladonna. Unfortunately, her head

seems to be easily turned by a future promise." Perpetua bowed her head. "It saddens me so that sister would turn against sister for the promise of a love that might not have ever belonged to her."

"Elsavetta, please explain to me what zippling involves and how it can be reversed."

Tremble moved her chair in order to give Elsavetta her complete attention. It seemed that the woman had lived quite a long physical life. Her silver hair was arranged in a bun that sat squarely on the top of her head, making it look like a small hat. While her beauty was still clearly visible, there were deep lines of worry that graced her face. Tremble wondered if the woman had experienced more sadness then some of the others.

"Zippling might be likened to cutting something up." Elsavetta's description made Tremble flinch at the thought of it happening to Forrest. "Oh, my dear, I am sorry. Not a literal cutting of flesh and bone, it would be the dissecting of his powers. It is very hard to explain. Each enchanter or enchantress is born with a certain amount of power. The amount depends on their heritage. You, obviously, have great powers because your parents individually have strong magic. As you age and mature, these powers advance and are enhanced by aspects that you learn and develop."

"If I may interrupt, sister, it would be quite similar to a mortal child's development. The child would be born with certain aptitudes because of his or her parentage. Education or training would develop the strengths the child naturally had."

Tremble nodded her head at Perpetua before returning her attention to Elsavetta.

"Zippling would have taken a portion of Forrest's powers and splintered them into multiple Forrests."

"Like cloning?" Tremble saw that several of them seemed confused by the term. "Cloning involves creating a genetic reproduction of a being without reproducing in the traditional sense. It is the creation of something scientifically rather than biologically."

"That is an interesting concept. I have not heard of it in our world." Elsavetta tilted her head as she spoke.

"It has been done in this world by your brother." All eyes diverted to Baldric. "No, by your brother, Amadeus. As Scordato, he has cloned himself. I know this for a certainty because such cloned versions visited me in the mortal world."

"Oh, good gracious! He dared to do such?" Abelia seemed the most shocked by the thought.

"He did not attempt to harm me. I gather that these clones are not as powerful as the original version."

"Yes, that example does describe what we mean by zippling." Elsavetta continued her story. "Zippling is more about power than having a physical self. By zippling Forrest's powers, his energies could be used in several different ways at once. It would make someone like Sebastian much more powerful than he actually could ever be on his own."

"Does this hurt Forrest?"

"In theory, it should not. It just depends on how long it goes on and if the magic is damaged in any way. It is vastly more complicated than my experience can fathom. It would have taken Sebastian finding Forrest in a state of having his guard down for him to be able to get this control or to have Scordato do this." Elsavetta paused as Verina whispered to her. "Yes, that is possible. Being in the mortal world would be an ideal time for that to happen. Tremble, do you know if Forrest ever physically visited you?"

Tremble thought for a moment about what Forrest had said to her when he made the appearance, with the physical features of Andrew, in her dreams.

"Oh, I believe he did. Shortly after I began to learn about my heritage, Forrest visited me in one of my dreams. He took on the human form of my father Andrew. It was comforting and upsetting at the same time." Several of the sisters nodded in understanding. "During that dream visit, he said that he had stayed as far away as he could only daring to touch my forehead once as I dreamed. I assumed that he meant while I was still a child. Could that have been when it happened?"

"I believe that would be a strong possibility, Tremble." Baldric's voice was somber. "The mortal world can be dangerous for enchanters. It is because there is not as strong of a combined magic energy in the atmosphere. Magic feeds magic, so to speak. That, combined with the fact that seeing his child for the first time would be a vulnerable emotional moment, is probably all that it took for Scordato or Sebastian to get close enough to Forrest's power to splinter it. Unfortunately, I believe it can only be reversed by the one who caused it in the first place."

"That is correct, Baldric."

"Another problem to solve. The list is continually growing."

"Alas, my child, it is so. However, fear not! The seven of us are ready to assist you."

All seven of the siblings stood as Perpetua spoke. They smiled broadly at Tremble.

"Please do not be offended. I do not understand how you can help me, though, in your present state."

"We still have our power, even if it is confined."

Baldric made a movement with his arm around his head that reminded Tremble of a cowboy twirling a lasso. Instantly, the entire scene burst into flames all around him. With the snap of his fingers, it disappeared as quickly.

A snowstorm began in Verina's frame. It whirled to blizzard intensity before a bright sun melted it all away.

Within Gwenora's area, hundreds of birds of all colors and sizes flew covering the background with a sea of multicolored feathers that became invisible with a nod of her head.

"Okay, I understand that you all still possess power. What about outside those frames? Show me what you can do."

"We thought you would never ask." Verina giggled with delight.

Each of The Seven began whispering. They made eye contact with each other before simultaneously snapping their fingers. Tremble felt her butterfly pendant float up off her shoulders and over her head. It hovered in the air before stopping in front of Perpetua. Within a few moments, Tremble watched as five other pendants appeared in front of their original owners.

Though Baldric continued to look, he soon let out a deep sigh and shook his head.

"I was afraid that my pendant would not come. Obviously, there must be strong magic hindering it."

Tremble looked down at the one that still hung around her neck. Amadeus' pendant lay perfectly still. She began to walk around to look at each of them. They all had a butterfly design each with a prominent color. Abelia's pendant was orange. Crispina's was yellow. Gwenora's color was fuchsia. Teal was the color for Elsavetta. Frilly pink fit Verina as her color.

"What color is yours, Grand?"

"The pendant that adorns the neck of your father is all the shades of blue imaginable. It is indeed a beautiful work of art. Our dear Inezia gave each of us the beauty of her heart when she created these pendants of safety."

"Do you think there is any possibility that I might be able to summon that pendant?" The idea sprang out of Tremble's mouth like a thought placed in her head.

"I do not think that you would be able to do so any more strongly than I can as the original owner of it."

Baldric's tone was sterner than Tremble had heard directed to her before. The expression on his face, however, showed that he was pondering the concept.

"Let's test that hypothesis." Perpetua nodded her head and extended her hand toward the pendant that dangled before her. "Call forth this one to you."

Tremble cut her eyes toward Baldric and peripherally also looked at the others. The sisters were all glued to the conversation.

"Okay. I am not sure what to say."

"Think about it, my dear. I am sure that your magical mind can conjure a command that will be appropriate for the task."

Tremble nodded to Perpetua. She began to think. Slowly, the words came.

"Pendant's power, long ago. Bestowed with love, for all to know. Created freely, safe from harm. Come to me, reveal your charm."

Everyone watched in silence. The purple pendant before Perpetua remained perfectly still.

"I did not think that it would be poss—"

Baldric's words were silenced as the pendant suddenly left its place in front of Perpetua and flew into Tremble's extended hand.

"Magnificent!"

Verina was the first to speak her delight as the other sisters began to applaud.

"We always wondered what the combined power of two of our lines might produce." Abelia seemed especially excited as she was jumping up and down. "It is glorious to see this. Simply glorious."

Baldric was silent, lost in thought. His scowl had changed to a look of shock.

Perpetua's smile was broad and full of pride. She laughed as she watched Abelia jumping in the frame beside her.

"Tremble, I think you should recite your spell again." Everyone stopped what they were doing as Baldric spoke. "Humor your old Grand."

"Sure, I can do that." Clutching the purple pendant in her hand, Tremble began to concentrate. "Pendant's power, long ago. Bestowed with love, for all to know. Created freely, safe from harm. Come to me, reveal your charm."

Tremble was not sure what her grandfather expected to happen. The pendant that she clutched in her right hand did not move. The one around her neck was also still. The other five still hung in the air before each of their respective owners. The scowl returned to Baldric's face. He shook his head and paced back to the corner of his frame area.

She had just turned to look at Cinnamon; the wizlet child was still sitting between Gwenora and Crispina's frames. The light above Tremble's head became brighter causing her to look up. She quickly moved as she saw that with great speed something was falling toward her head. Tremble barely got out of the way before the object reached her and stopped in midair.

"I would not have believed this story." Verina's words broke the silence.

"I most certainly would have."

Perpetua's voice, which had sounded older to Tremble up until this point, had the lilt of youth in it. Baldric returned to view and clapped his hands in delight.

"There it is! My old friend indeed."

Before Tremble was the bluest butterfly she could have ever imagined. The shades were mesmerizing and calming while also being bold and regal. The pendant looked like it belonged around Baldric's neck. This butterfly was a manly warrior. Her mind quickly left the color as a thought entered.

"What does this mean for my father? If this pendant has left his possession, has his safety been compromised?"

"Tremble, I understand where your concern would come from. Remember though, that your own mother gave up her pendant and remained safe." Baldric's tone was gentle. "I would not have encouraged you to call it forth had I thought that it would jeopardize Forrest even further. We must accept the fact that we do not know how safe Forrest is. If what you say is true, his power has already been splintered. The charm of this pendant did not stop that from occurring."

"Take it, Tremble. He wants you to have it."

Tremble looked deep into her grandmother's eyes. There were many lifetimes of wisdom and understanding contained within them. Slowly, she reached out and grasped the butterfly with her left hand. Both of her hands lit up with a powerful glow. Tremble unclasped her fingers and held the two pendants side by side in her open hands. The shades of blue and purple sparkled like a light show. Soon, she saw that all of the other pendants were doing the same. All, but the one that hung around her neck.

Chapter Thirteen

"I WOULD HAVE THOUGHT there might have been even a miniscule connection." Perpetua's somber words seemed to echo the expressions on her siblings' faces. "I suppose he has truly been dead to us, and we to him."

"It is time for you to go and meet your destiny, young lady." Baldric changed the uncomfortable subject. "We want you to take all of these pendants. If you wear all of them together, there must surely be a mass of power that can help you defeat The Evil. All of these pendants are infused with the magic and love of Inezia. As the child of the most powerful enchanter to have ever graced our world, these tokens possess unimaginable power. We wish that we could accompany you on the rest of your journey. Alas, that ability was taken from us long ago. This is what we can do. Put them all around your neck. Feel their weight. Feel their enchantment and protection. Know that we are with you."

Looking around the room at all of their eager faces, Tremble began to feel her fear depart replaced by a renewed conviction to overcome what was ahead.

"You can do this, Princess Tremble. I see it in your heart. I feel it in your spirit." Cinnamon rose from her hiding spot and began to fly around Tremble's shoulders. She thought she felt something like sparkles falling from the child. The little girl giggled, "Wizlet dust makes you brave."

With a renewed strength inside, a smile on her face, and wizlet dust on her shoulders, Tremble took first the purple one, followed by the blue, and put them both around her neck. Nothing happened to the green one that had belonged to Amadeus, but the other two hummed with excitement.

"Has anyone ever wore these together?"

"Not to our knowledge." Perpetua looked around at the others as she answered. "You are the only person in this family who has ever possessed more than one of these pendants. I doubt that it would have even occurred to us that it could be done until we saw that you had mine and Amadeus' on together."

Cinnamon tugged on Tremble's sleeve. The little one was smiling and shaking her head positively.

"You can do this. You are supposed to be the one."

With all the centuries of power that surrounded her, it was this tiny little being who gave Tremble the most confidence. She took a deep breath and reached out for the next closest necklace. As she put that one on, the luminous glow increased. With each successive one, the light grew brighter and the weight around her neck grew heavier.

Tremble had not realized that she was putting them on in order of age until she reached the last pendant, Verina's pink one. The enchantress gave her a smile that could have easily glistened a movie screen. For an instant, Tremble could see a young woman who bravely travelled through time to save the man she had loved from afar. As Tremble returned the smile, she hoped that there was another side to this journey that would allow her to hear the woman's incredible story.

"It is beautiful."

Eight butterflies all hung from chains around Tremble's neck. Within moments, the colors were flashing as if they were attuned to their own music. Only the one that had been created for Amadeus, the green one, remained unlit.

"All of us together as one. It is a happy and sad moment."

Tears flowed down Perpetua's cheeks as her arms tried to reach out to her siblings. Even after the long years of confinement, Tremble saw how their hearts yearned to embrace each other.

It was Cinnamon who announced the arrival of someone by poking Tremble's leg. She followed the little girl's gaze as the visitor walked toward them.

"Inezia."

All eyes shifted to the corner of the room as Inezia slowly walked toward them. Tremble dared not look at the siblings as she could surmise from the sounds she heard the shock that was filling the room.

"We have not seen you since—"

Perpetua's words were stifled by the sob that followed. Tremble realized that she was about to witness the releasing of hundreds of years of emotion by all of the siblings who were old enough to have known and remembered this nanny to them, this aunt.

"Hush my children, no tears. I have shed enough for all of you for more years than I can count." Inezia's voice was soft and gentle with its own layer of emotion just under her edge of control.

"How did you come to be here at this present point?" Baldric's tone almost sounded childlike. "You have never graced our presence in all these many years."

"I could not risk it. Sebastian surely knows the state that all of you find yourselves in. Yet, he has chosen to leave you alone. My presence with you might aggravate him. He hates to see me happy. Gazing upon your faces now is one of the happiest moments I have had in a hundred years."

A chair appeared underneath Inezia as she began to crumble to the floor. Tremble did not seem to have the ability to move from her spot; she was glued to watching all that was transpiring. It was tiny Cinnamon who fluttered over to the old woman and sprinkled wizlet dust upon her.

"Why have you come now?" Baldric asked his question again.

"I could feel when all of you summoned your butterflies. I knew that something important was happening. You were doing something for Tremble, and I might be able to help."

"Why didn't you bring my mother with you?" Tremble came out of her haze.

"Once again, it was a risk. I left an illusion of myself with Jasmine so as to try to divert attention away from coming here. I do not know if it will work. Since Sebastian's powers are not his own, he might not be able to tell the difference."

"We thought if we gave our pendants to Tremble, it would give her enhanced protection." Perpetua's voice grew stronger.

"Indeed, it shall. I cannot imagine what might result from all of the pendants being on one person."

"If my neck does not break first from the weight of them."

No sooner did Tremble make her comment than Inezia's hand went up in a fast movement. Tremble felt for the pendants as she could no longer feel the weight of them. All were still safely there.

"I think it is time for Tremble to go forth and face her foe." Inezia stood up from the chair and walked back toward the group. The seven frames were as close together as they could possibly be. "How I wish that I could embrace each of you!"

Inezia's sadness weighed heavy on Tremble's heart. Taking in a deep breath, she looked down to see that Cinnamon was watching her and reached out to take her hand.

"Oh, Princess Tremble, before you go, you must dance with me."

"Cinnamon, I am not that good of a dancer and besides, I doubt there is time—"

"There is always time to dance." Cinnamon began to twirl. The action lifted the little one up into the air.

"Yes, Tremble, there should always be time to dance." Inezia winked as she responded.

Tremble took Cinnamon's hand and began to dance with her. Looking around at the portraits, the sisters were all nodding. Baldric was shaking his head back and forth, but a smile graced his face.

"Very well then, it appears I am outnumbered."

Tremble began to move her feet in small movements across the floor.

"You must twirl, Princess Tremble. Twirl like me!"

Tremble began to mimic the movements of her little friend. She twirled and twirled. The portraits moved back and gave her added room. Tremble continued to twirl around the room. Glancing down, she noticed that multicolored sparks were flying from her fingertips. The pendants began to flash brightly. Ghosts of the butterflies that hung around her neck flew up above her toward the ceiling. She was so mesmerized by everything. She kept twirling. All of a sudden, she was so dizzy she fell to the floor.

Tremble watched as the cluster of ghost butterflies flew to each painting. In a line, the butterflies flew around the circumference of each frame. Tremble watched as a purple glow began to flow from the edges of Perpetua's frame. One by one, the same thing happened to each in their respective colors. The last being the blue that came forth from Baldric's portrait.

The butterflies returned to the pendants around Tremble's neck. She felt a jolt of magic pass through her as each of them returned. As she looked back toward the portraits, she was amazed to see that Perpetua was stepping out of the frame. Baldric followed suit. The two stood side by side, half in, half out, and looked at each other. Shock and amazement passed over their expressions. When they had both successfully come out of their prison, they motioned for their five sisters to do the same. Each enchantress held long within the bounds, stepped out of the frames. Gwenora, the sister who had spent the longest in captivity, squealed with delight as she joined them.

"It is a miracle." Gwenora's words were choked in emotion. "I will be able to hold my baby in my arms." Gwenora looked around. She saw Tremble. "Until then, you, my dear, will do just fine."

Gwenora held her arms open wide. Tremble got up from where she had fallen and ran into her waiting embrace.

"Is this the real reason you came, Inezia?" Baldric was the first one to break the silence as the siblings embraced each other.

"Honestly, Baldric, I had no idea this was possible. I have hoped that once the prophecy was concluded that you might be freed from this bondage. I did not expect it to be this way."

"What shall happen to us?" Verina's question made all of the siblings stop what they were doing. "We physically died."

"It is obvious that Scordato's spell was able to stop that physical process and extend your immortality." Inezia's response brought smiles to the faces of the sisters.

"That's something that I have wondered about myself." Tremble left Gwenora's side and walked over to the others. Each of the sisters grabbed hold of her as she passed them. "If enchanters are immortal, why do they die at all?"

"Such a wise one, our Tremble is, so discerning." Perpetua released Abelia from their clutching embrace as she spoke. "Magic is not a cut and dry, black and white, type of power. There are layers to the process and vast exceptions to every rule on which it is based."

"A mortal's days are numbered. From the day he is born, the clock starts ticking and the time will run out. An immortal has no such clock, but another can take his life force or alter it with a magic that is shrouded in evil intent." Abelia took a turn pulling Tremble into an embrace. "The strength of your determination and vastness of your power has helped to make this miracle possible. Yet, it is more than that. It is much more. It is the—"

"The pureness of her heart." Cinnamon's soft voice spoke from a distant corner.

"It was you." The knowledge hit Tremble, all at once. "It was you. You knew that this could be done. You knew that if you made me twirl—"

"Your magic is special, Princess Tremble. You don't know how to get it out yet. I must help you."

"We must all help Tremble." Baldric walked to the center of the room. "We shall defeat The Evil that has torn up our family. It is time for us to go back to where it all started. We shall go to the Garden of Stone and face the devil among us."

There was no further discussion, no time to prepare. Tremble watched as Perpetua and Baldric lifted their arms up toward the sky. The butterflies lit up around Tremble's neck and their ghosts flew toward a ceiling that was no longer there.

"Join hands." Perpetua's direction caused everyone to scramble into a circle. "Tremble, come stand between Baldric and I."

"What about Cinnamon?" Tremble looked around for her little friend.

"Cinnamon shall come with us." Inezia motioned to the wizlet. "She shall travel between myself and Verina. We shall keep her safe."

Tremble watched Cinnamon scamper to Inezia. Her little friend joined hands with Inezia and Verina before looking back at her with a wink and a nod.

As Tremble moved toward Perpetua and Baldric, two voices whispered in her head.

'It's time.'

UNLIKE THE OTHER journeys Tremble had made in Neverwrong, there seemed to be no passage of time with this one. With Perpetua on her right and Baldric on her left, they joined hands. Instantly, they were following the ghost butterflies up into the sky.

As quickly as that happened, Tremble again felt her feet on the ground. The view in front of her was familiar—The Garden of Stone. Before her stood the statues of Marcellus and Claudia. Five of their daughters were huddled around them, not daring to touch their loved ones. Perpetua and Baldric were huddled by a tree in deep conversation with Inezia. The leaves above their heads showed hopeful expressions, as if they anticipated something grand was about to happen.

Tremble realized that she was standing all alone within an arm's length of the back of the two brave young men who had accompanied her on this journey. Mortal and immortal, there was no difference now as they stood in stone silence.

Just in front of them hovered Cinnamon. The little one was vainly sprinkling wizlet dust on Laken and Jake. She whispered something to them. Tremble was about to walk toward them when a voice beckoned from behind her.

"Tremble, please come here." Jasmine called her daughter.

Tremble briefly looked at those who came with her. They were not aware that she was wandering into the edge of the forest.

"Mother, where are you?"

"I am here."

Just a few feet away, in a cluster of trees, Jasmine stood. Her aura was a deep, royal blue. It radiated all around her. Tremble felt one of the butterflies around her neck begin to vibrate. It was the blue one, the one her father had given up just a short time earlier. Jasmine held out her hands to Tremble. Something about the action made Tremble weary. She stopped for a moment.

'It is me.' Jasmine's voice whispered in her head to answer her concern. 'You have become so wise and discerning.'

As she continued to walk toward her mother, Tremble began to see that she was not alone. A few feet behind her was the translucent form of a man—a tall, dark, handsome man. Tremble recognized immediately that he was a younger version of her Grand, Baldric. It was Forrest.

"We probably only have a few moments, my child." Jasmine's normally strong voice quivered. "We want to have this time with you."

The translucent form of Forrest joined Jasmine as Tremble drew closer to them. His smile was broad and proud, yet, in his eyes, Tremble saw a sadness that overpowered any happiness he might have felt.

"This is your father, Tremble. This is Forrest."

Tremble gazed into his eyes and saw a recognition that could only come from genetics. As there was not a memory for her to retrieve from any other time. Forrest looked down at himself and met her eyes again.

"This is what is left of me. I am a warrior in pieces. I am an enchanter of science who cannot devise a spell to put himself back together again." Forrest extended his arms to Tremble and put them back down again. "I long to encircle you and your mother in a family embrace. It is a feeling I may never experience."

"Never?" Tremble looked from Forrest to Jasmine. "Why is he saying never?"

"This spell that has splintered your father into his present state is an ancient one. Sebastian drew from the very powers and bindings of Meserve to create it."

"I thought that Sebastian couldn't actually perform the spells himself. That is why he has been using Scordato or Belladonna."

"That is true. He performed this spell on your father through Scordato. It wasn't Scordato's power alone that accomplished it. This is what makes it all the more improbable to overcome."

"I will not die in this state, my daughter. But, I will not be the enchanter that I once was either. I cannot help you fight this battle. My powers are limited."

Tremble put her hands over her eyes and concentrated. She was being bombarded with so many thoughts that her brain felt like it might burst forth and escape her skull.

"I have a legion of power with me now. These ancestors of ours are simmering with pent up power and aggression. None of them will go down without a fight."

"I have no doubt of that, Tremble." Jasmine pulled Tremble's hands off her face and looked deeply into her eyes. "You must remember that it is not their battle to fight. There is a mighty force in your corner. I shall be there, as will others."

"Ultimately, it is up to me." Tremble let out a soft chuckle. "I am the fulfillment of the prophecy. There's no time like the present."

Before Jasmine or Forrest could utter another word, Tremble turned on her heels and walked straight back into the garden. Her concentration and resolve must have shown itself in the atmosphere as everyone turned in her direction.

"We have assembled here for a purpose and there is no reason to put it off any longer. This is the day of fulfillment for the prophecy." Tremble paused and searched the group. Her gaze rested on Perpetua and Inezia. They were standing side-by-side. "How do we call Amadeus into our midst? How do we reach beyond what he became and communicate with who he was?"

The two enchantresses looked at each other. Tremble knew there was a conversation going on that no one but them could hear. Moments passed without an answer from them. It was Baldric's voice that broke the silence.

"Have Perpetua sing to him. It will draw him to this place like a moth to a flame." Baldric looked around at the others. "Before some of you existed, Pet would sing to Amadeus and I, at night, before we went to sleep. It was one of our most favorite things."

"My dear, Baldric, I sang the songs of our parents' youth. They were songs that were taught to me by our mother and Inezia. They are songs in another language—the language that came in the earliest of times."

It began as a whisper, a melody more beautiful than the grandest of orchestras. The words were incomprehensible to Tremble, and yet, on some level, she understood them completely. Her eyes travelled around the group and she could see that everyone was lost in the music. Most mesmerized of all was the young boy in the man named Baldric. His expression was as if he was in ecstasy.

It was Cinnamon who alerted Tremble to the entrance of Scordato. The childlike expression on his face spoke volumes. His reaction had been just as Baldric predicted. He was pulled to the garden by Perpetua's melodious voice.

Perpetua's eyes had been closed for most of time as had the sisters' while they listened. As if she could sense his presence, her eyes slowly opened. She continued to sing as her eyes darted to those who she wished to understand what was occurring.

"Your voice is every bit as lovely as I remembered. My heart feels at home for the first time in centuries."

Before Perpetua or any of the others could react to him, Tremble walked toward Scordato.

"We were hoping that would be your reaction. It is time for you to have a family reunion."

"Ah, the precious Tremble, heir to the throne, fulfiller of the prophecy. I am so happy that this time has come for us to meet again. I was beginning to think that you had skipped the other aspects of the prophecy and were busy turning your back on your homeland."

"Certainly not. You have done a better job of that than I could ever dream of doing."

Tremble walked around in a small circle. The action gave her the opportunity to make eye contact with a few of the others, especially Baldric and Perpetua.

"Our dear Laken was slacking on his history lessons if that is what you believe. I was the one who was left for dead while I still lived. They all but admitted to it when I last was reunited with my siblings."

"That is where your misguidance began, my dear brother." Baldric walked up and stood beside Tremble. "Your memories have been tampered with by the one who has been influencing you all along."

"Is it back to this tactic again? How many times must I tell you people? No one is influencing me."

"Really? So how is it then that you knew how to work a spell that would splinter your own nephew into magical pieces?" Perpetua joined Baldric. "Inezia tells us that it is not in any of those precious books you have so carefully read in the Library."

"The old woman must be mistaken. I had to have gleaned it from—"

"The old woman is right here, and I happen to have been the keeper of those books before you were even a twinkle in your father's eye, young man. You have been influenced, controlled, and used by the most evil being our magical kingdom has ever known. It started when you were just a wee lad."

"But, I—"

"Did I say you could speak, Amadeus? You must remember what I have taught you. You speak when you are asked to speak and you do not interrupt an elder."

The whole fairy godmother persona that Tremble had thus far imagined with Inezia was totally replaced at that moment by the image of a mean grade school principal.

"Yes, ma'am."

A quick glance at Scordato revealed that he thought the same thing as Tremble. He was in full school boy form. She could see the beads of sweat on his forehead.

"I can prove it to you."

Inezia walked over to Scordato. With just her index finger, she taped his forehead. Brilliantly colored sparks flew out of her fingertip as she began her spell.

"Memory, memory, we used to know. Come out from hiding and put on a show."

Rays of light burst forth and the scene around them immediately changed. They were in the Library. A young and pale looking Amadeus opened up the lid of the shelf seat where he had been placed. He looked around the room. Slowly, he raised himself up and climbed out. As he lowered the lid back down, he collapsed onto the seat that had been hiding him. Amadeus put his face in his hands and began to cry.

"Oh, little one, do not fret. Your Uncle Sebastian is here to help you."

Tremble heard gasps from some of the sisters, but it was Scordato's reaction she was most interested in.

"They have left you. It is shameful. You were so sick. The healing touch of your dear sister brought you back from the brink." Tremble saw a smirk cross Scordato's face. "I will tell you the truth of the matter. It will all be folly later as I manipulate your mind; you will never remember this. I daresay that was not of Perpetua's knowledge that her touch had such power. Her mother's healing was widely known to bring many an enchanter back from certain death. I will tell you later that it was Baldric's envy of his twin that allowed him to leave you here. The pain in your brother's heart will never cease. It will turn him into a shell of his former character. He will be riddled with the guilt for being the one who survived. The only reason that they have departed today is because your pitiful father warned them I might find all of you one day. What he failed to tell you is that the name that would summon me was laid bare in these very books you and Baldric have so carefully scrutinized. Marcellus' own sons summoned the one who would take his life. I thank you for your assistance. You will continue to help me until I take control of everything your father so dearly loved."

With a snap of Inezia's fingers, the scene changed back to their present setting. Scordato stood with all eyes upon him. His pallor had changed and reminded Tremble of the Scordato that she was first shown, frail and in rags.

His eyes did not focus on any of them. He stared straight ahead as if he was searching his mind for an answer that he knew was not there. In a flash, they were back in the same room again. This time, it was a memory that *he* had chosen. As it came into view, it was the scene that Verina had taken Tremble to see. All of his siblings were beseeching their brother to believe that he had not been left as living. A young Verina pulling on his coattails with talk of a special song made Scordato end the scene abruptly.

"I do not understand." For the first time, he looked directly at Baldric and Perpetua. "I do not understand any of this. It is not as I have been—"

"Told?" Baldric finished the sentence. "Your memories were altered, my brother. Altered by the one who has been set on destroying our family from the very beginning."

"A short time ago, I told you that your pendant would one day come back to you." Inezia moved toward Amadeus as she motioned for Tremble to follow her. "I said that one day, the giver of it would free you from the bonds that held you."

Tremble took Amadeus' pendant from around her neck. Inezia nodded and Tremble gently slipped the chain over his head. For a brief second, their eyes locked and she felt the ground move below her feet. Stepping back, Tremble watched as Baldric and Perpetua drew closer to him. Confusion passed over Scordato's face. It was as if two people were warring within him. Slowly, Baldric and Perpetua encircled him. Tears filled his eyes as he looked at each of them. Closer they came until they were fully embracing him. The five other sisters joined all around until Tremble could no longer see him.

"Watch closely."

Inezia was behind her. Tremble felt Jasmine's arms grasp her waist from behind. She felt the butterflies pulsating around her neck and could see all of the colors sparkling together. Tremble saw the bold green color of Amadeus' pendant shoot up from the center of the embracing siblings and heard Scordato cry out in pain.

All of the siblings backed away and the oldest of them stood alone. As he turned to face Tremble, she saw a stranger. His features were the same, yet he looked different. No longer was he the evil enchanter Scordato, Amadeus now stood before them.

"We do not have much time. I do not know how I know this. I am certain, just the same. There is something that I must do. Something to remedy some of the evil I unknowingly have done."

Amadeus motioned for everyone to step back. He began to quickly twirl. Tremble remembered that she had seen him do this when he had changed from rags to finery during that first fake memory she had seen in the Library. This time, he chanted a simple spell, over and over again.

"Reverse, reverse, turn back to one, everything that I have done."

The words passed his lips at least ten times before the spinning slowed. Thunder crashed in deafening decibels. The view grew dark and multicolored lightning lit up the sky. Frightening moments passed. Tremble felt someone on each side of her take her hand. When the light of day returned, Tremble looked around her. All of the siblings were doing the same. Amadeus was nowhere in sight. Inezia and Jasmine were holding her hands.

"Where is he?"

Jasmine did not verbally respond, she just pointed in the direction of the statues. Amadeus stood with his back to them. From the angle where Tremble was, he was blocking the view of where Laken and Jake stood in stone. Tremble released their grasp and ran over, stopping in her tracks as she saw what remained.

Laken smiled at her. He was flesh and blood again. Beside him, there was nothing.

"Where is Jake? What happened to Jake?"

Tremble's heart raced with fear. She looked at her mother. Jasmine's brow was furrowed. Behind Jasmine stood CeCe. Tremble hadn't realized that the guardian was even present.

"CeCe, where is Jake? What happened? I don't understand."

"I was the one who put Jake into your life." Her answer came from Amadeus. "Laken was right when he tried to divert him from your attention. I took this mortal and made him a distraction. I was pleased to see that you had chosen to bring him with you on this journey. I would have used him to my advantage."

"A distraction? A distraction!" Tremble felt an ache in her heart. Sobs welled up in her throat. "How could you? Bring him back! Bring him back!"

Tremble lunged for Amadeus. To her, he was every bit as evil as he had always been. Laken jumped between them and put his arms around her to hold her back.

"I cannot bring him back. He was in your life at my bidding and for my purpose. I have undone all of the evil that I committed."

"He was not evil." Tremble's voice sounded like the hiss of a snake. "He was a good man."

"He was my pawn in your life."

"That's hardly an answer." Jasmine took Tremble out of Laken's arms. "You should have thought of *all* the consequences before you undid all of your work, before you took away Tremble's love."

"Love? How dare you speak of someone taking away love!" Belladonna swooped down from the top of a nearby tree. "You can now watch your daughter feel the pain that I endured at your hand."

All Tremble could see through her tear-soaked eyes was the blurry outline of Belladonna and the glimmer of the red diamond pendant. The pain and rage that was building inside began to make her heart pulsate and she felt faint.

"The mortal would have never survived what Sebastian had planned. He was spared an agonizing death unlike my love who painfully died." Belladonna approached Jasmine and Tremble. "This daughter of yours will right your wrong though, my darling sister. She shall make me whole again."

Belladonna leaned over and looked straight into Tremble's eyes. Belladonna's pupils were as red as the diamond around her neck. The diamond that was infused with The Evil. Tremble focused her mind on the spell she was trying to cast. She had to be silent, cautious like a cat. As she finished, the red diamond slipped off the necklace and into Tremble's waiting hand. Whispering another spell of concealment, Tremble let her body go limp and she fell out of her mother's arms and to the ground.

"Always the center of attention, ever since the moment of her birth."

From the sliver of opening that she allowed her eyes to have, Tremble could see Belladonna walking away. Jasmine had knelt beside her and placed a hand upon Tremble's forehead. She began to feel her mother's healing pass over her. It was warm and calming.

'I am fine.' Tremble's mind whispered.

'I know you are. This will ease your shattered heart. I am so sorry about Jake.'

The loving words of her mother awakened a new round of crying within Tremble. She could no longer pretend to be unconscious. A hiccupping sob rose out of her.

"The precious princess is indeed awake. It is time for you to reverse the act of love that killed my beloved. I have waited long enough."

Tremble had barely rose to her feet before she saw Meserve appear behind Belladonna.

"The child shall do no such thing. The act cannot be of anyone's choosing but that of her own."

"Old man, your interference is not welcome here."

In a flash, Belladonna turned to face Meserve, her right arm was extended with her finger pointing straight at him. She moved her left hand toward her neck to clutch the pendant that was no longer there.

"Where is it?" Belladonna looked down at the empty chain. "Who has taken my diamond from me? Jasmine, you must return it."

"Jasmine does not have it, my faithful one." All eyes darted to the voice that came from behind the statues of Marcellus and

Claudia. "It is our darling Tremble who used a cunning spell to slip it off your neck. I am most impressed with your talents, my dear. I shall not forget that when I am making assignments in my new kingdom."

Tremble began to lunge toward Sebastian. Forrest's voice calmed her. 'Not yet.'

"You shall make the child bring back my Xavier or I shall destroy the child. Without her, My Lord, you can never fulfill your destiny."

Belladonna moved toward Tremble. It did not take long for Jasmine to move between them.

"I have loved you for your entire life, my sister. I have trusted you with everything that is dear to me. I know that it was my hand that caused you your greatest pain. But, that was never my intent. You have planned to use my daughter from her very birth. You have been a party to the imprisonment and splintering of my husband. You have made a deal with the devil and now dare to threaten my child's existence in my very presence. I have no more use for you. Our parents aptly named you. You *are* a deadly poison!"

It seemed to Tremble the next few moments were in slow motion. She watched as her mother turned her back on Belladonna. Her aunt extended her hand as if to administer a spell toward Jasmine. Her mother was too quick for her. Jasmine whirled around and reached out her arm toward Belladonna. The most powerful force Tremble had yet to see shot out of her mother's fingertips.

"Obliterate!"

It only took one word for Belladonna to be gone.

"MY POOR BELLADONNA, she so naively thought that her love would be returned. It was not in my plan."

Since he had arrived, Sebastian had remained behind Marcellus and Claudia. As he spoke, he walked around to the front of the statues and looked at them closely.

"It has been a long time, Marcellus. You do not look well. You are very grey. But, Claudia, you were always the kinder of the two. You hardened your heart against me though. Oh wait, no, it was *I* who hardened *your* heart." Sebastian howled with laughter.

"How dare you speak of them? How dare you even breathe in their presence?"

Baldric held his brother back as Amadeus rushed toward Sebastian.

"Amadeus, it is such a shame that this family reunion of yours opened your eyes to my plan. I had every intent of allowing you to assist me in my rule. Tsk, tsk, tsk. Now your betrayal will be rewarded with the punishment of you watching each of your siblings die. The younger ones are such innocents really. I shall start with them. I want Baldric and Perpetua to watch, too."

Sebastian walked toward Verina. Tremble could feel the red diamond materialize in her clutched hand. A voice that she did not recognize spoke to her. 'You must destroy the diamond. It is the only way to end him.'

"Why are you bothering with them?" Tremble stepped forward and Sebastian turned on his heels. "I am the one who you have to defeat in order to get what you want. You took a gentle land, a humble yet powerful people, and put them in a state worse than death. I shall right those wrongs. I shall free them. Come and meet your destiny." Tremble opened her hand, palm up, and showed Sebastian the red diamond. "Does this mean something to you?"

"Precious Tremble, stop making idle threats. We all know that you are not going to do anything with that beautiful jewel. I am sure that at the least one of these enchanters has told you that the stone is the source and core of all of Meserve's power. Since all of you descended from him, it is your source of power as well. If he dies, his magic dies with him."

"Yes, Sebastian, you are right. That is what I was told. I have been schooled better than you can imagine though."

Tremble began to pace back and forth in front of Sebastian. She threw the stone up in the air and caught it as a child would throw a ball.

"Here's the thing though. Being *the* heir of Neverwrong, I have had some unique opportunities. I was able to read passages of books that were written by Meserve just for me. I know things that no one else knows but him. The destruction of this stone will kill you and Meserve, no doubt. It will not, however, destroy all the power of the Royal Family of Neverwrong."

"Silly girl, I am the master of deception, you cannot deceive me. I know that you are bluffing."

Sebastian began pacing in the opposite direction that Tremble was going. Like guards outside a castle, they turned and marched back toward each other.

"I speak only the truth. Only one other being can vouch for this knowledge—the one who made it so."

"Prove it."

"Sebastian, those might be some famous last words. Surely, you do not want our battle to end so easily."

"Our battle shall not end until I say it does. You will not do it. You are not brave enough."

Tremble tasted Sebastian's words and anger washed over her. For a split second, she was a little girl again who was not allowed to watch her favorite television show. The same dogged determination rose inside her, yet, the image in her memory brought a smile to her face as before her eyes she saw the first man she had ever loved —Andrew Dawson—her father smiled and nodded as the voice of the other father she barely knew whispered in her mind. 'It is time.'

Tremble looked to those who were standing all around her— The Seven plus the brother they had left behind, Inezia, CeCe, Laken, and her beautiful mother, Jasmine. Beyond them, she saw the stone statues of those who had created this family she now knew to be her own. Beside them was a space of dust, the memory of her first true love. Sitting to the side, taking it all in was the most powerful enchanter that the magical world had ever known. She realized, as she gazed upon him, that it was his voice that had spoken to her earlier. It was his words. 'You must destroy the diamond. It is the only way to end him.'

Summoning all of her courage, Tremble raised her hand and threw the diamond to the ground as one word left her lips.

"Obliterate!"

With one word and one motion she did what no one else could do.

The diamond shattered into a million pieces. A deafening cry left Sebastian as the voices of hundreds simultaneously yelled out with happiness. Tremble could not see it, yet she knew that Inezia's homeland was whole again. The melancholy had been peeled away and the spirits of her people had been returned to their bodies. With one final yelp from Sebastian, The Evil disappeared. All that remained of the diamond was a tiny piece of stone that Tremble picked up and held in her hand.

Tremble turned to look at Meserve and found that Inezia had kneeled at his feet. It was obvious that his time was ending. Tremble listened to his whispered voice.

"Tell them the prophecy that I have shared with you."

"And the magic shall pass from the old one as an heir destroys The Evil. From the first heir shall there one day be a King."

"It is time for that to be fulfilled. But not before I share with you one last thing." Meserve motioned for Tremble to come near him. She knelt before him and he grasped her hand. "The virtuous ones can only be freed by a tremble of light from another time. You, my dear, are that tremble of light. It is why I gave my darling Jasmine your name."

Tears rolled down Tremble's face as she now realized what she must do.

"I shall reverse an act of love."

"You will indeed. I shall not see it, but it is my greatest wish."

Tremble rose from her spot as Meserve once again motioned for someone to come to him. She watched as a hesitant Laken walked toward him.

"It is time for you to become King. It is time for you to carry the power of Neverwrong."

Meserve pulled Laken toward him and placed a kiss on his forehead. Lightning flashed through the sky. The ground shook and rumbled. When all was again silent, Meserve was gone.

Tremble watched The Eight as they beamed with pride at the sight of their new king. There was no sadness, only a feeling of completeness. Looking over her shoulder, she saw that Jasmine was walking toward her. A few feet behind her, from within the woods, came the handsomest man Tremble had ever seen. She would one day learn to call him Father. For now, she was content to run into his embrace and feel the love of the parents whose love gave her an extraordinary life.

"There is no greater love than the sacrifice a parent makes for a child." Inezia's words brought Tremble back to what she must do. "Jasmine and Forrest made a great sacrifice to insure your safety. Yet, long before they existed, there were two parents who knowingly walked into a living prison to shield their children from The Evil."

Tremble walked toward Marcellus and Claudia. It was all coming back to them.

"For hundreds of years, you have endured a torturous existence that only few can imagine." Tremble looked at Laken. His expression was full of understanding. "It was the ultimate act of love that put you here. It is time for me to reverse that and for you to return to your family."

Tremble hesitated. It was CeCe who helped her have the courage to understand.

"You know how to do this."

A smile crossed Tremble's face as she took a deep breath.

"I want Marcellus and Claudia to return to their family!" Tremble lifted her arms up to the sky.

The clouds opened above them and a bright light shone down.

The virtuous ones were freed by a tremble of light from another time.

"YOU HAVE HAD the power to return to the mortal world all along, my dear. You have always had the power to wish yourself anywhere."

In true fairy godmother fashion, Inezia flicked her wrist and Tremble's ensemble changed to 'travelling clothes,' as she called them.

Tremble looked at those who remained around her. Marcellus and Claudia were reunited with their children. Jasmine and Forrest could finally enjoy a life together free from the worry of lurking evil. Scordato was no longer the forgotten one as Amadeus was made whole again with the love of his family. His son, Laken, had been promoted from Protector to King. The others would go back to the normal life of Neverwrong. Tremble was not sure what that was.

It was indeed a group of people with whom she would forever have a connection. In a world that was now her heritage. But, her 'heart's desire,' as Dorothy once said, was to be in the arms of the woman who had raised her and feel the comfort of what would always be her true home.

Tremble's mind journeyed back to one of her last memories before she left her mortal life. 'Choo Choo and I will be sleeping right here while you are gone.' She could see Dana curled up in her big bed with the little poodle snuggled beside her. Taking one last look at her new family, Tremble took a deep breath and closed her eyes.

"I wish that I was home in my mortal world!"

Tremble did not need any ruby slippers to get her back to her mother's house, the home she had grown up in. As instantly as she said the words, she was there.

"IT IS JUST AS I expected."

Tremble stood at the doorway of her bedroom. Cuddled in her bed, lay Dana and Choo Choo. Upon hearing Tremble's voice, her mother rose so quickly from under the covers that Dana's feet tangled causing her to fall over the side of the bed.

"Oh, oh, you are here. You are really here!"

Dana tried to untangle herself and get to her feet. Before she could do so, Choo Choo was jumping all over Tremble, forcing her to sit down on the floor. Dana crawled over and joined them.

"I was afraid I would never see you again."

Choo Choo yelped as Dana's hug trapped the dog between the two of them.

"You know us college kids—we are always going off on some wild summer adventure."

"Oh, Tremble, how can you joke like that?"

"I can joke like that because it is over. It is finally over."

"Tell me everything."

TREMBLE WASN'T SURE how much time passed. They had moved from the bedroom to the kitchen downstairs as Tremble told her mother every detail of her time in Neverwrong—the good, the bad, and the utterly frightening. Dana's animated reactions to Tremble's story were comical at moments as her mother prepared her favorite dinner with all sorts of utensils flying through the air with her mother's gasps of surprise at the more shocking details of Tremble's story.

It was after they had eaten and were huddled on the couch in the living room that she got to the part about Jake, Dana broke down in sobs causing Tremble to do the same.

"Oh, my darling, it is awful. I don't understand why Jake could not be spared."

"I don't really either. When Scordato tried to undo all of his evil, Jake was a casualty of that. He was only in my life as a distraction—a distraction that I loved with all my heart." Tremble wiped her nose on her shirt cuff. "After that happened, I was so afraid that I would come back here and find that Choo Choo was gone, too."

"Not our Choo Choo. She is real. We met her mama, remember?" Dana gave the poodle a scratch behind the ears.

"Yes, it does appear that she was not a creation of his. It makes me so happy. I'm never going to forget Jake though. He was my first love and that's special."

"Indeed it is."

They sat in silence for a few moments, snuggled together on the couch.

"What happens now, Tremble?"

"I don't know, Mom. I know that I belong in that world. It is a part of me now. My head tells me that. My heart though wants to be here with you and Choo and VeVette. I want to make a real life here. Maybe CeCe and Bridget will let me work at Kaleidoscope."

"It's funny. Before Bridget left, she said that she hoped for that very thing." Dana got up and walked toward the kitchen. "Oh, I have your phone charging over here. It looks like you have a message."

"Right now, I want to take a shower. Wash all the Neverwrong dust out of my hair. You find us a good movie out of Dad's collection."

"*Practical Magic*, perhaps." Dana chuckled as Tremble rose to go upstairs.

"Only if we can have midnight margaritas."

As Tremble walked toward the counter where her phone was charging, she reached into her pocket and pulled out the small piece of red diamond.

"I brought back a souvenir from Neverwrong." Tremble laughed to herself.

"Tremble, you never told me what the name was that Sebastian had taken from Inezia's homeland. You told me how you learned it. You didn't have to use it though, did you?"

Tremble looked back over her shoulder at her mother. Sitting there on the couch looking happy and rested, Tremble could almost see Andrew sitting beside Dana trying to work the VCR so that they all could watch the movie. The memory made her smile. She pushed the button to play her phone message as she began to answer Dana.

"It was a really simple name, full of history. The name was Maya."

"Tremble, this is Jake. What happened? Are you alright? How did I get back home?"

The ground rumbled under Tremble's feet. She dropped the phone. The lights went out. Darkness filled the room.

"Tremble? The breaker must have thrown. There's a flashlight in the drawer there. Tremble?"

"And his name shall be Scordato, the forgotten one.
He shall overcome those who have forsaken him.
A child shall be his deliverance from captivity.
A child of power shall free him from the bonds of e
vil and be a light of renewal. He shall not perish if his
heart is pure. The child shall be the heir to all things.
The heir shall reverse an act of love.
The mightiness shall cease."

ACKNOWLEDGEMENTS

Inspiration comes in a variety of forms. For me, my deepest inspirations came out of my childhood. My love of reading and good movies was cultivated from birth by my parents. We would read and watch grand adventures. These two things were as common in our home as a meal on the dinner table.

I've always said that I blame by imagination on being an only child with older parents. It was fueled by the fact that I lived in a neighborhood that was basically devoid of children—at least ones of the age and common amusement to interest an imaginative little girl. I created my own friends and we had great adventures. Those friends are still with me today and they venture out, from time to time, through my fingertips in the words of my stories.

Now that this trilogy has concluded, I will share with you—my readers—that one of the characters of this story is in honor and celebration of a dear friend from long ago who died way too young. Behind the character of Laken was the image of a real-life friend of mine. He left a distinct impression on my life and was the beginning of my love of the color purple. Sadly, he was taken my cancer a few years ago. This series is dedicated to his memory.

In the previous two volumes of this series, I have acknowledged the significant impact that several dear friends have made on the creation of this story. I am deeply indebted to my following special readers and editors for their careful wisdom and guidance: Pam Newberry, Carole Bybee, Marcella Taylor, and Donna Stroupe. My eternal thanks and appreciation goes to each of you.

Cassy Roop with Pink Ink Designs has gone above and beyond to make this cover and the formatting of this manuscript a delightfully creative process. I hope one day soon we can meet face to face.

I have been blessed with a patient husband. I am thankful for his strength and understanding as I travel down these creative roads pursuing my dream of writing. I am glad that he is with me on this real life journey.

ABOUT THE AUTHOR

Rosa Lee Jude began creating her own imaginary worlds at an early age. While her career path has included stints in journalism, marketing, hospitality & tourism and local government, she is most at home at a keyboard spinning yarns of fiction and creative non-fiction. She lives in the beautiful mountains of Southwest Virginia with her patient husband and very spoiled rescue dog.

The Enchanted Journey is Rosa Lee's second series. She is also the co-author of the award-winning time-travel series, the Legends of Graham Mansion. Learn more about her writing life at RosaLeeJude.com.

www.ingramcontent.com/pod-product-compliance
Lightning Source LLC
Chambersburg PA
CBHW032051260626
47157CB00020B/2794